SUMMER OF FREEDOM

Also by Oliver Hilmes

Berlin 1936: Fascism, Fear, and Triumph Set Against Hitler's Olympic Games

Franz Liszt: Musician, Celebrity, Superstar

Malevolent Muse: The Life of Alma Mahler

Cosima Wagner: The Lady of Bayreuth

Summer of Freedom

HOW 1945 CHANGED THE WORLD

Oliver Hilmes

Translated from the German by

Jefferson Chase

Other Press | New York

Originally published in German as *Ein Ende und ein Anfang: Wie der Sommer 45 die Welt veränderte* in 2025 by Siedler Verlag, Munich

The translation of this book was supported by a grant from the Goethe-Institut.

Production editor: Yvonne E. Cárdenas
Text designer: Julie Fry
This book was set in Aldus and Kabel.

10 9 8 7 6 5 4 3 2

 Printed in the United States of America on acid-free paper. For information write to Other Press LLC, 267 Fifth Avenue, 6th Floor, New York, NY 10016. Or visit our Web site: www.otherpress.com

Library of Congress Cataloging-in-Publication Data
Names: Hilmes, Oliver author | Chase, Jefferson S. translator
Title: Summer of freedom : how 1945 changed the world / Oliver Hilmes ; translated from the German by Jefferson Chase.
Other titles: Ende und ein Anfang. English
Description: New York : Other Press, 2026. | Originally published in German as Ein Ende und ein Anfang : Wie der Sommer 45 die Welt veränderte in 2025 by Siedler Verlag, Munich. | Includes bibliographical references.
Identifiers: LCCN 2025042293 (print) | LCCN 2025042294 (ebook) | ISBN 9781635425413 hardcover | ISBN 9781635425420 ebook
Subjects: LCSH: World War, 1939–1945—Peace | World politics—1945–1955
Classification: LCC D816 .H5513 2026 (print) | LCC D816 (ebook)
LC record available at https://lccn.loc.gov/2025042293
LC ebook record available at https://lccn.loc.gov/2025042294

It's good that this beast has finally been laid low, but what damage has it done!

Alfred Döblin, May 1945

The Third Reich ended up in ruins and rubble. This bust of Adolf Hitler was found near Berlin's Potsdamer Brücke bridge.

AT THE ABYSS

When Harry walks down the hallways of his new home, he gets the feeling of being at sea. The floor creaks under his steps and seems to move like the deck of a rolling ship. Chandeliers weighing half a ton begin to swing, and the crystal glasses on the table clink together. Again and again, the heavy curtain sways as though directed by an invisible hand while mysterious groans emanate from the venerable walls. You might think that Harry is imagining this. Perhaps his nerves are gone or his fantasy has run wild. But Harry's senses aren't deceiving him. His new domicile is in fact in disrepair, and unless something is done in the foreseeable future, it could collapse like a house of cards. The building in question is the White House.

In November 1944, Harry S. Truman ran for Vice President of the United States of America alongside Franklin D.

Roosevelt. It was the fourth time Roosevelt had put himself up for America's highest office and, again, his ticket won. A few months later, on April 12, 1945, FDR suddenly died, making Truman president. Former First Lady Eleanor Roosevelt gave him, his wife Bess, and his daughter Margaret a tour of the presidential residence.

"The White House looked splendid from the outside," Margaret would remember. "But the private quarters were anything but comfortable in those days. It was not unlike moving into a furnished apartment, where no new furniture or equipment had been purchased for twenty or thirty years. The furniture looked like it had come from a third-rate boarding house. Some of it was literally falling apart."[1]

Mrs. Roosevelt assured the new inhabitants that the place would look much better with a fresh coat of paint on the walls. Margaret chose Wedgwood Blue for her living room and pink for her bedroom. Bess Truman preferred blue for her bedroom and gray for her living room, while her husband's bedroom was painted beige. The couple obviously slept apart. The Oval Office was made over in off-white. On May 7, the renovations were completed. That very day the Trumans moved into their quarters in the White House.

As the movers carry hundreds of boxes into the building, and a crane hoists Margaret's grand piano into the second floor, President Truman learns from General Dwight D. Eisenhower, Supreme Commander of the Allied Forces in Northwestern Europe, that Colonel General Alfred Jodl of the German Wehrmacht has capitulated at Eisenhower's headquarters in the French city of Reims. Because Jodl has argued that the Wehrmacht leadership needs time to communicate the order to surrender down through the ranks, it has been agreed that Germany will officially cease hostilities the following day. Truman thus spends his first night in the White House secure in the knowledge that the Second World War will be coming to an end, five years, eight months, and seven days after it began.

When Truman awakes at the crack of dawn on May 8 in the presidential bedroom, he no doubt has little desire to think about the physical state of the building. A press conference, to be broadcast on the radio, is planned for 9:00 a.m. Word has gone round that the new president has something very important to communicate to the American people, and the press jockeys for position when White House spokesman Jonathan W. Daniels admits reporters into the Oval Office at 8:35. Also present are Bess and Margaret, Truman's cabinet, and ranking American and British military commanders and congressional leaders. They're seated on chairs ringing the president's desk. The journalists have to stand. It's so crowded that someone could pass out without hitting the floor.

Truman tells those in attendance that what he's going to announce is top secret until 9:00 a.m. But it's so brief, he adds, they'll all have plenty of time to write their reports. The reporters laugh. Truman jokes that it's also a special day for him personally. He's just turned sixty-one. "Happy

Following Germany's unconditional surrender, US President Harry S. Truman prepares for his radio address, in which he will announce the end of the Second World War in Europe. "This is a solemn but glorious hour."

Birthday, Mr. President," someone calls out. Then the clock strikes nine, and Truman begins to speak.

"This is a solemn but glorious hour," he says. "General Eisenhower informs me that the forces of Germany have surrendered to the United Nations." He points out that the Second World War isn't yet over and done with and that Japan and the United States are still locked in a terrible battle in the Pacific. He warns the Japanese that, from now on, the full might of the American military machine will be directed against them. The press conference is over in minutes.[2]

While Truman accepts further birthday congratulations, shakes countless hands, cuts a huge cake, passes pieces to his closest staff members, and at some point goes back to work, New York prepares for what is by far the biggest American celebration of V-E Day. Masses of people gather in Times Square, getting ready for the tens of thousands of celebrants who will march down Fifth Avenue to showers of confetti. All in all, half a million people take part. But by evening, the city returns to its normal hustle and bustle. "Yesterday's news had hardly any effect on the theatrical box offices last night," the *New York Times* reports the following day. "Ticket booth attendants said that there were some seats canceled, but they were immediately snapped up by other buyers."[3]

How long has the German novelist Alfred Döblin waited for this day? How often has he imagined a gigantic sinkhole opening in the ground and sucking Adolf Hitler down to the depths of hell? Twenty times? Thirty? More? Döblin can't say. "It's good that this beast has finally been laid low, but what damage has it done!" he writes to friends in May. Some sixty million people have died, civilians as well as soldiers, and nine million men, women, and children have been murdered in the concentration camps and death camps, including six million Jews. Broad stretches of the European continent have been devastated.

In Los Angeles, the city in which Döblin sought refuge five years ago, he notes: "Perhaps my exile will be over in a few months—but what comes next? Life is a series of adventures."[4]

V

A good week after Adolf Hitler's suicide in the bunker of the Reich Chancellery, wild rumors are swirling around Berlin. "Hitler is in Japan, in Spain, near Hamburg, he's shot himself, and he has fallen in the battle for the Reich Chancellery," Else Tietze muses in her diary. Her real name is Elisabeth Anna Henriette, but for as long as she can remember, everyone just calls her Else. She doesn't quite know what to make of all the talk. "If God granted him a soldier's death, He would have done very well by him. I still believe that the man wanted to do good, but he must have gone insane at the end."[5] Mrs. Tietze insists that she was never a true National Socialist. On the other hand, the Russians were Germany's enemies. Nonetheless, when she walks through the streets of the Reich capital now, she doubts Hitler more and more. "You almost get the feeling that Hitler only wanted to leave his enemies a completely destroyed Berlin and didn't even think about the poor, unhappy people."[6]

Else Tietze is in her early seventies and lives in a stately apartment in Holsteinische Strasse, not far from Stubenrauchplatz square in the district of Steglitz. Her husband, Richard, a retired colonel, died three years ago. The people in her building, which has miraculously survived the war without major damage, address Else as "Mrs. Colonel," which always makes her particularly happy. Her Richard was a respected man, she thinks. People held him in high regard, and some of that now seems to have rubbed off on her a bit.

The Tietzes had three children—Traute, Hildegard, and Richard Junior—but Else hasn't heard from them in several weeks. When the Red Army reached Berlin, Traute and her husband, Hans, fled head over heels to southern Germany. They'd heard that Stalin's troops usually made short work of members of the SS like Hans. Else's son, Richard, followed in his father's footsteps and joined the army. He's said to have been fighting in Potsdam—there has been no trace of him since. Her daughter Hildegard is the only one Else knows is safe. She married a piano maker and emigrated to the United States in 1933.

"Our longing and worry are sometimes too much," Else complains more than once these days.[7] It gnaws at her not to know how the children are doing. Although she has previously never spoken much about her feelings, to say nothing of putting them in writing, she has been keeping a diary for a few weeks. It's her "intimate journal," a place to confess the fears and worries that torment her, as well as her fragile hopes. If Traute and Richard are still alive, she wants to give them her diary someday. Until then, Else records her experiences as best she can. On May 8, she writes: "The children are already playing happily in the street here again, and on my way today, which took me past many Russian vehicles, I saw a Russian cutting a thick slice of bread for a boy who accepted it with a smile. Incidentally, they have scores of horses, most very good-looking, not small Russian horses, but beautiful, large ones. No doubt they were all stolen and confiscated German ones."[8]

May 8, 1945, is a busy day at Buckingham Palace. At 11:00, there is the usual changing of the guard, a ceremony that has continued uninterrupted throughout the war. At the same time, King George VI is handing out "Distinguished Service Medals" and "Military Medals" to 270 soldiers who acted with bravery beyond the call of duty. Around noon, Prime Minister Winston Churchill arrives in a civilian vehicle to have lunch with the monarch. When the crowds that have congregated in front of the palace recognize him, the police have to restrain them. The seventy-year-old leader is the man of the hour, the person regarded as the driving force behind the Allied victory over Nazi Germany, and now that peace is finally at hand, the British people want to celebrate with their prime minister. After lunch, Churchill returns to 10 Downing Street to deliver a radio address. "We may allow ourselves a brief period of rejoicing, but let us not forget for a moment the toil and efforts that lie ahead," he says. "Japan, with all her treachery and greed, remains unsubdued. The injury she has inflicted on Great Britain, the United States, and other countries, and her detestable cruelties, call for justice and retribution."[9]

Meanwhile, the crowd in front of the palace has swelled to some one hundred thousand. Cries of "We want the King!" go up, at first individually, but soon as a collective chant. Then the balcony door opens and for the first time that day King George VI, Queen Elizabeth, Princess Elizabeth, and Princess Margaret appear before their subjects. The king wears a Royal Navy admiral's uniform, and Princess Elizabeth fatigues from the "Auxiliary Territorial Service," the women's division of British Army, which she joined earlier in the year. Queen Elizabeth and Princess Margaret are both dressed in blue.

Churchill is on his way from Downing Street to the Ministry of Health in Richmond House. There, on the balcony, he makes another speech. "My dear friends, this is your hour," he calls out to the crowd. "This is not victory of a party or of any class. It's a victory of the great British nation as a whole... Now we have emerged from one deadly struggle—

a terrible foe has been cast on the ground and awaits our judgment and our mercy."[10]

The celebrations know no bounds. All in all, around two hundred thousand people take to the streets. Later that afternoon, the king has an official audience with Churchill and the members of the War Cabinet in the Bow Room, where official receptions are held. At 5:30 p.m., the royal family returns to the balcony to greet the crowds, this time alongside the prime minister.

V

Over in Paris, as Truman and Churchill are speaking to the American and British peoples, Charles de Gaulle, the head of the provisional government of the French Republic, addresses his compatriots. "The war is won," he proclaims in an emotionally trembling voice on the radio on May 8 at 3:00 p.m. "Victory is here! It is the victory of the United Nations and the victory of France!" At the end of his speech, the general gets carried away with his own pathos: "Honor to you! Eternal honor to our armies and their leaders! Honor to our people who wouldn't be weakened or bent by terrible tests! Honor to the United Nations, which mixed their blood with our blood, their pain with our pain, their hope with our hope, and which triumph today along with us. Vive la France!"[11]

But these words have been preceded by a fierce quarrel between Washington, London, and Paris. Originally, de Gaulle wanted to announce victory independently on May 7. Downing Street was taken aback, and British diplomats sent cables to the general urging him to abandon the idea. De Gaulle is considered completely unpredictable. "If, however, he was unwilling to accept this advice," one sober diplomat concluded, "no further pressure could be brought to bear on him."[12]

Wounded pride is a major reason for de Gaulle's behavior. Roosevelt and Churchill declined to invite him to the major war conferences in Tehran and Yalta, and ever since he has mistrusted the Americans and the British. Roosevelt considered de Gaulle a would-be Napoleon who would try to misuse the war as a springboard for a dictatorship. Churchill thinks much the same. "He hates England and has left a trail of Anglophobia behind him everywhere," the prime minister told his ministers back in May 1943.[13] "He has never himself fought since he left France and took pains to have his wife brought out safely beforehand." Churchill described de Gaulle as "vain and even malignant" and suspected him of having fascist tendencies. More than once, the prime minister quipped, "Everyone has his cross to bear—mine is the Cross of Lorraine," referencing the symbol of the French Committee of National Liberation. And Stalin? The Soviet leader has scoffed that the French general behaves like the head of a great nation, when in reality he has very little power.[14] There is obviously no love lost between these two men either.

After his speech, the fifty-four-year-old heads to the Arc de Triomphe to lay a wreath at the Tomb of the Unknown

Soldier. As he tries to leave the massive memorial, the masses surge forward and trample all over the symbolic grave. Otherwise, V-E Day proceeds in orderly fashion. For the first time since the start of the Second World War, Paris is equal to its reputation as the "City of Light." The city's landmarks are illuminated; the opera house shimmers in the French national colors, blue, white, and red. "Everyone seemed to be everywhere," remembered one person present. "Jeeps, trucks, both civilian and military were packed with people, both civilian and military. I don't think any jeep had less than twenty people on it and trucks as many as they could hold and more. Flags were flying from the vehicles; horns were blowing and everything sort of gave the impression of a huge informal Fireman's Parade."[15]

Airplanes circled over the city center for hours, dropping confetti and streamers. Spectators watched breathlessly as an American Mitchell bomber succeeded in flying underneath the Eiffel Tower. Again and again, the crowd sang the Marseilles: "Allons enfants de la Patrie, le jour de gloire est arrivé."

What a day! Late that evening, reflecting on events, Churchill can't stop thinking about the conflict with de Gaulle. He takes a pen and paper and jots down a telegram, marked personal and top secret, which he sends at five minutes to midnight to the British ambassador in Paris, Duff Cooper. "We must discuss the visit of the general here later," Churchill writes. "It may well be that I could go and see him quietly one of these days on a trip to France, though I should have to know beforehand that he would not have the door banged, barred and bolted against me."[16]

V

At the end of the Second World War, the men and women at Berlin's Main Statistical Office count 245,300 buildings in the city, of which 27,679—or 11.3 percent—are totally destroyed. 8.2 percent of buildings are badly damaged, and 9.3 percent repairable. The remaining 171,965 (70.1 percent) have suffered only slight damage and are habitable.[17]

The raw numbers are one thing. The disastrous impression that the devastated city makes is another. Even specialists are filled with dismay at the mountains of rubble. When the famous architect Hans Scharoun is asked how long it will take to clear Berlin of debris, he takes a long drag on his cigar. "Around fifty years," he says thoughtfully, blowing smoke up at the ceiling. "After that reconstruction can begin."[18]

V

As the world celebrates the end of the "beast," Adolf Hitler, and the final demise of his empire of terror on May 8, 1945, two young men drive a US Army Jeep from Innsbruck across the Austrian-German border into Berchtesgaden. Behind the wheel is Grayson B. Tewksbury, a photographer for *Stars and*

Stripes. A short time later, on Bavarian soil, the two men leap out of the vehicle. This is a particularly special moment for the passenger, who had to flee Germany in March 1933 to avoid being arrested by the Nazis. Now, twelve years later, he's back in the country as an American citizen. His name is Klaus Mann.

The thirty-eight-year-old son of Nobel laureate Thomas Mann is here to report from liberated Germany and neighboring countries for *Stars and Stripes*. Wherever he goes, he speaks with locals, interviews people of influence, and writes accounts of his travels for the US military newspaper.

But on his first day back in Germany, before Klaus Mann begins his work as a correspondent, he seeks out a bit of very personal past. He and his family used to live in a luxurious villa on Poschingerstrasse in Munich's Bogenhausen neighborhood, which Klaus and his siblings affectionately referred to as "Poschi." Driving there on the Autobahn, he and his friend Grayson imagine what it would be like to ring the bell and have some Nazi bigwig open the door. "Mr. Obersturmführer shall be hereby advised that this villa is the legal property of my father," Klaus intends to proclaim. "Mr. Obersturmführer is to vacate the premises. I'm giving him two minutes."[19] The two men rub their hands in glee. But when they arrive in Munich, the mood sours. The sight of the devastated city is too grim. "Munich is no longer there," Klaus will report to his father a short time later. "The entire center, from the main train station to Odeonsplatz square is nothing but ruins."[20]

When the Jeep turns on to Poschingerstrasse, Klaus initially breathes a sigh of relief. His family home is still standing. The three-story house seems to be unoccupied, and the front door has been nailed shut. There's no trace of any Nazi bigwigs. When he forces his way in, he's amazed at what he sees. New walls have been put up everywhere, dividing the once impressive rooms into small spaces. Klaus is unable to find a single intact piece of furniture: Everything is in pieces. In the overgrown backyard, he discovers a young woman who has made a makeshift shelter on the second-floor balcony attached to his former childhood room. She refuses to tell Klaus her name when he asks. She looks at him skeptically, perhaps because she's puzzled that a GI would speak such good German. Finally, she informs him that she's been bombed out and lost her entire family, including her fiancé, in the war. Klaus asks her if she's aware of who owns the villa. She can't say anything about that, she responds in the broadest of Bavarian accents. She's heard that the house was used by the *Lebensborn* organization. Klaus has no idea what she's talking about. "Strapping young men from the SS were here, very fine individuals," she explains. "Purebred steers. That's what they were used for. As steers and stallions. Because of their racial pedigree—you understand?"[21]

Pacific Palisades is roughly nine thousand kilometers as the crow flies from Munich. This lovely part of the world—

calm, mild of climate, always green and full of small, curving streets—is one of the better parts of Los Angeles. For four years, Klaus Mann's parents Thomas and Katia have been living at San Remo Drive 1550. They were forced to flee Germany when the Nazis came to power in 1933 and eventually arrived in the United States after time in Switzerland and southern France.

May 8, 1945, is an exhausting day for Thomas Mann. He's accustomed to a hearty breakfast ("tea, two eggs with the white of one removed, and toast with honey"), then a bath and usually a walk through the neighborhood streets, but today he leaves the house on an empty stomach.[22] V-E Day celebrations are already underway on the East Coast, but Katia drives her husband to Beverly Hills where the famous writer has an appointment for a comprehensive medical examination. For a year, he's been losing weight and has complained of a recurring nighttime cough and chronic gastroenteritis—maladies for which no cause has ever been determined. X-rays are to be taken to shed some light on his conditions. Physicians give him a contrast medium to drink, then the procedure begins. In the afternoon, after a midday break during which Mann is allowed to return home but told not to consume any food, more X-rays are taken. "In the car some vermouth and a cigarette," he notes in his diary when the procedure is over. "At home, soups, pork chops, and coffee."[23] The causes of Thomas Mann's ailments will never be determined.

That evening, Thomas and Katia sit down before the radio to listen to a recording of President Truman's speech.

Although Mann is tired from the medical examinations, among other things, and doesn't feel like celebrating, he opens a bottle of champagne to mark the occasion. In his diary, he notes: "The Russians are still searching in vain for Hitler's body."[24]

V

"To a man, everyone is proud of what he achieved in five years of war," complains writer Erich Kästner, whose works were branded "degenerate" by the National Socialists and publicly burned on Berlin's Opernplatz in May 1933.[25] "Down with decadence and moral decay!" a student had shouted as he threw Kästner's novel *Fabian* into the flames. Propaganda Minister Joseph Goebbels despised authors of Kästner's sort, whom he regarded as representatives of a decadently urban "asphalt literature." Nonetheless, Kästner was still able to earn a living despite an official publication ban by writing a few screenplays for the National Socialist film industry under pseudonyms.

The forty-six-year-old is in no mood to celebrate on this day of surrender. Kästner believes it's a bit self-rich for the Second World War's victors to blame Germans for being too weak to escape from the yoke of Nazism. "Who made a pact with the executioner Hitler when he had long been publicly showing himself in our country?" he asks in his journal. "It wasn't us. Who concluded the concords? Signed the trade agreements? Sent diplomats with congratulations and athletes to the Olympics in Berlin? Who shook hands with the criminals instead of with the victims? Not us, gentlemen. You hypocrites!"[26]

Erich Kästner writes himself into a rage. He has no doubt that the Allies are sweeping their complicity in National Socialism under the rug: "The victors who put us in the dock should sit down beside us. There's plenty of room on the defendants' bench."[27]

The Russians are here! At around 9:00 p.m., engines can be heard approaching. Startled people stand at their windows, peeking out fearfully. They can see Red Army tanks and trucks driving past, waving red flags and flares. Although the soldiers on the vehicles are armed, they don't look dangerous. More and more men, women, and children come out onto the streets to cheer them. The soldiers wave back. The Russians are here! These few words spread like wildfire on this May evening through the old North Bohemian fortress, located northwest of Prague at the confluence of the Eger and Elbe rivers, which the Nazis turned into the Theresienstadt concentration camp in 1941. More than one hundred forty thousand people—including around fifteen thousand children—have been interned here under the most inhumane conditions.

Margot Bendheim is among those completely overwhelmed by events. The twenty-three-year-old Berliner has been a prisoner for a year, and it's here that she's gotten to know Adolf Friedländer, eleven years her senior and a casual acquaintance in Berlin. The two have recently become a couple. Margot and Adolf are all alone in the world. In December 1942, Adolf's mother, Fanny, was sent to Auschwitz and murdered. Margot's mother, Auguste, and brother, Ralph, suffered the same fate a month later. Adolf's sister, Ilse, is said to have fled to the United States via Italy, but he has no idea whether she's still alive.

Margot and Adolf head to the camp entrance when the Red Army reaches Theresienstadt that Tuesday evening. The gate is wide open, and the dreaded guards have disappeared. The two of them could just walk out, but they stand rooted to the spot for some minutes. Is this a dream? Could this really be happening? They take a few tentative steps forward and suddenly find themselves on the road to Prague. "Adolf was standing next to me," Margot will remember, "We looked at each other. We experienced the liberation together. It's a moment we will never forget."[28]

Although ecstatic crowds in London, Paris, and New York have been celebrating the Allies' victory over Nazi Germany for twenty-four hours, it's strangely calm in Moscow. Life goes on, one might think, and as if to prove it, that afternoon Russian state radio broadcasts a fairy tale. Stalin has decided to treat the declaration of surrender in Reims as a merely "preliminary document" to be superseded by an "act of general and unconditional capitulation" to the supreme commander of the Red Army in Germany's headquarters in Berlin. Stalin justifies this demand by saying he's afraid that Wehrmacht units in the east might not abide by the ceasefire, but that's just a pretense. His actual motivation is prestige. The "real" capitulation should be made to a Soviet commander—after all, the Red Army has made the greatest sacrifice in the war. The original plan of announcing the end of the conflict simultaneously in Washington, London, and Moscow is moot. Stalin wants a "victory day" of his own on May 9, and what Stalin wants, Stalin gets.

In the night between May 8 and 9, the capitulation on which Stalin insists takes place in Marshal Gyorgy Zhukov's headquarters. The setting could hardly be more symbolic: a building used until recently as an academy for Wehrmacht cadets and for a training center for military engineers. There, the war is declared over for a second time. Taking part in the event along with Zhukov are Marshal of the Royal Air Force Arthur Tedder, US General Carl Spaatz, and French General Jean de Lattre de Tassigny. The German delegation consists of Wehrmacht Supreme Commander Field Marshal General Wilhelm Keitel, Navy Admiral Hans-Georg von Friedeburg, and Luftwaffe Colonel General Hans-Jürgen Stumpff.

Hundreds of reporters and photographers anxiously await the moment when Zhukov orders the German commanders to appear in the building's ballroom. The delegation enters, and Keitel raises his marshal's staff in greeting. Zhukov asks him if he has read the capitulation agreement, and Keitel affirms that he has. The Soviet marshal tells the Germans to approach his table. "Keitel quickly rose, shooting a malign glance at us," Zhukov would recall. "Then he lowered his gaze, slowly picked up his Field-Marshal's baton from the table and walked unsteadily to our table. His monocle dropped and dangled by its cord. His face was covered with red blotches."[29] Amidst a storm of photographers' flashbulbs, first Keitel, then Friedburg and Stumpff sign the five copies of the capitulation agreement. Afterward, Zhukov and the other Allied representatives put their signatures to this document, ending the ceremony. When Keitel notices his adjutant breaking into tears, he hisses audibly: "Stop that. After the war, you'll earn a fortune if you publish a book entitled 'My Life with Keitel in a Russian POW camp.'"[30] The clocks read forty-three minutes past midnight.

"Suddenly all of the tension drained from the ballroom," one eyewitness will recall. "A general sigh of relief and exhaustion makes itself felt. Germany's capitulation is sealed. The war is over."[31] Once Keitel, von Friedeburg, and Stumpff have left the ballroom, Zhukov has an opulent dinner with vodka and champagne served. In an adjacent building, the Germans are also presented with a banquet of no less fancy hot and cold dishes. "For dessert there were frozen strawberries, which I had never eaten in my entire life," Keitel later says in praise. "Apparently a Berlin gourmet restaurant supplied them. The wines, too, were of German origin."[32]

Around this time, the lead announcer of Radio Moscow, Yuri Borisovich Levitan, sits down at the microphone to announce what is already known around the rest of the world. Within minutes, crowds of people, many still in their nightshirts swarm the streets of the Soviet capital, joyously chanting, "Victory, victory!" Some weep while others pray. That evening, a thousand cannon shots are fired, and then Stalin addresses his people. "Three years ago, Hitler proclaimed, at a volume impossible to ignore, that his goal was to shatter the Soviet Union and take away the Caucasus, Ukraine, Belarus, the Baltics, and other territories. He openly declared: 'We will destroy Russia so completely that it will never be able to rise again.' That was three years ago. Hitler's insane ideas would not become reality. The war blew them away in all the four winds. In fact, the exact opposite of the scenario that so enraptured Hitler's supporters has come to pass. Germany has been utterly defeated. The German forces have capitulated. The Soviet Union is celebrating victory, although it has no intention of either splitting Germany into pieces or destroying it." A period of peaceful development in Europe will now commence, Stalin adds. "Let there be eternal fame for those heroes who have fallen in battle against the enemy and given their lives for the freedom and happiness of our people."[33] Stalin doesn't say a word about the Western Allies.

V

At some point on May 9, while Moscow is celebrating victory over Nazi Germany, Svetlana picks up the phone and calls her father. As she dials the number, the nineteen-year-old thinks back to her last encounter with him. It was the previous year, when Svetlana told him that she wanted to marry her boyfriend, Grigori. "May the devil take you—do whatever you want," the old man replied, declaring that he never wanted to meet his son-in-law.[34] Even when she became pregnant a little later, her father showed no enthusiasm. "You need some fresh air," he said tersely and sent her to his dacha. So, understandably, Svetlana is now a little afraid of talking to her old man, who can be so terribly bossy and ruthless.

"Papa, congratulations on your victory!" says Svetlana when her father picks up the phone. "Yes, victory," he replies thoughtfully. "Thank you, congratulations to you, too. How do you feel?"[35]

Svetlana stammers a few words, then bursts into tears. Like so many others, she is completely overwhelmed by the events.

That evening, Svetlana and Grigori invite lots of friends over to their apartment to celebrate. The vodka is flowing freely, and despite the crowd, the guests still find somewhere to dance.

Svetlana hasn't invited her father to the event. The other guests wouldn't have had as much fun if Josef Stalin were around.

V

Alfred Misselhorn was the "Führer's" last hope. He never met Hitler in person nor did the latter ever assure him of his highest regard. No, Alfred Misselhorn only knew Hitler from the radio and from the speeches of his commanding officers, who ceaselessly preached that Germans born in 1928, as Alfred was, were the final chance for victory. It was teenagers who had to succeed in turning the tide of the war. Alfred was only sixteen years old when he was called up in mid-January 1945 and taken to a sleepy village called Ober-Pritschen in Lower Silesia. He and his young comrades didn't have to fight there. "The military situation was catastrophic," Alfred would later recall. "Since the fall of 1944, it had been almost quiet on the eastern front." Just over a week after his arrival, the young soldiers were ordered to march west. What followed was a chaotic retreat through central and southern Germany, ending in Straubing in Bavaria. No one knew what to do with the juvenile soldiers or cared about them there. "I might as well have stayed at home," thought Alfred, staring at the deserted parade ground. Suddenly someone shouted across the square at him: "Don't you know how to salute?" Alfred looked around in astonishment and recognized a man in uniform. "It was a narrow-minded stickler of an administrative officer with a huge sense of his own importance. Probably never left the barracks. We have no more fighting men, but the military administration is still functioning."

At the end of April, Alfred is captured by the Americans and, after some back and forth, transferred to Würzburg. There, on May 7, he's crammed with sixty other German soldiers onto a freight car normally used to transport coal. The men are packed so tightly together that there's no sitting down. When the train starts to move, Alfred has no idea where they're being taken or that the journey will last almost two days. The train rumbles slowly down the tracks and stops again and again. The next day, Alfred turns seventeen, but he only thinks about his birthday once.

On May 9, the doors to the train car finally open. An American soldier orders them to get out and lay out the men who have died during the trip on the platform. "There was a long row of them," Alfred will remember. "The platform was just big enough." But where in God's name has he ended up? Somewhere he reads the name "Zotzenheim." Alfred and his comrades are about 10 kilometers northeast of Bad Kreuznach. Mainz, the next largest city, is around 30 kilometers away. "I felt really nauseated. The march went past the train station over the tracks into a field. We're not the first ones. You can see slumped figures to the left and right of the path."

The German soldiers' trek ends outside the neighboring village of Bretzenheim, where American forces have erected a three-meter-high barbed wire fence around an area of roughly 210 hectares. The camp within it serves as a holding pen for around one hundred thousand prisoners, who are now waiting to be distributed to other facilities. As beautiful as the landscape is in this part of the Rhineland, its vineyards and valleys lush with spring greenery, the camp is like hell on earth. The inmates sleep on the bare ground, exposed to the elements. There are no sanitary facilities, nor is there sufficient food or adequate medical care. "Three times a day it's 'dead men to the gate,'" Alfred notes in his journal. "The commando has a lot to do."

One day, out of sheer hunger, Alfred eats unripe fruit from a tree, resulting in severe diarrhea. Once he has recovered, he realizes: "I have to get out of here to stay alive."[36] But will he succeed?

On May 10, Orest Nikolayevich K., a major in the Soviet military justice apparatus, writes to his sister Natalka about his experiences in Berlin: "The city center is badly damaged, ruins upon rubble, rubble upon ruins, most of them old. American and British bombers have done a thorough job here. The outskirts of the city are essentially intact, women and citizens walk the streets and look you in the eye, trying to ingratiate themselves. They sweep the streets clear of broken bricks and iron. They now need to do the work themselves because they no longer have any Russian slaves [...]. With our beautiful, dark blue car, looted of course, we drive on to Alexanderplatz square. Our first stop. We then take photos at the Brandenburg Gate and at the Victory Column, not far away is the monument to that funny old man, Frederick 'the Great,' who took a pasting from Russian generals way back when."[37]

V

On May 11, Klaus Mann scores a real coup. The scene of this curious event an out-of-the-way villa in Augsburg, on whose well-manicured lawn twenty to thirty American, French, and British reporters, together with a handful of high-ranking officers, await probably the world's most famous POW. Hermann Göring, the self-styled last of the Renaissance men, arrives in a silvery gray uniform and a tent-like overcoat. Göring loves making big impressions. He's been known to appear dressed entirely in white, or light blue, or in a reddish-brown doublet with a puff-sleeved shirt and green boots, carrying a spear, striding through his pompous country estate in the Schorfheide region north of Berlin and feeding meat to the lions he kept there. There he hung works of art stolen from all over Europe in his gigantic entrance hall. Göring was Hitler's number two but once the tide of the war turned against Germany, he preferred to go hunting than visit the front. But in Augsburg, the Renaissance man has been cut down to size. "Disappointingly, I found him to be much less of a blob than I expected," writes Klaus to his father. "A man of just about average height with a fat belly

In May 1945, Hermann Göring is taken prisoner by American soldiers. Among the Allied journalists who questioned him outside a house in Augsburg is Klaus Mann: "Disappointingly, I found him to be much less of a blob than I expected."

and a double chin, but nothing monstrous about his features. You can't even say he seems particularly unlikable. On the contrary. Of course, there is a certain brutality about his expression. His eyes also gleam rather maliciously. But his voice is almost pleasant-sounding, solid and bright, if a bit fat, and his facial features are not badly formed."[38]

Göring enjoys the attention he's shown and dutifully answers the journalists' questions. He totally fell out with Hitler some time ago, he tells them. "Completely estranged!" he emphasizes with a raised finger. "Please stress that! It's important!" While the interpreters translate his words into English and French, he takes stock of the journalists. A bit of absurdist theater ensues.

"What about the concentration camps?" someone asks.

He had no idea what went on there, Göring responds. It was all Heinrich Himmler's doing. "If I had known about such atrocities, I would have protested and intervened!"

The conversation turned to the Reichstag fire in late February 1933.

"I wasn't involved," Göring insists with a grin.

In the end, Klaus Mann speaks up, addressing Göring directly in German, which seems to momentarily discomfit him. He obviously didn't expect an American soldier to speak to him in his native tongue. Göring has no clue that this GI is the son of Thomas Mann. "Is Hitler dead?" Klaus wants to know. The question is the subject of considerable controversy. For days, rumors have swirled that Hitler escaped Germany and is now on the lam. Göring immediately answers: "Yes. Hitler is dead. Without question! Beyond doubt!"[39]

V

Around this time, the New York newspaper *PM Daily* asks Thomas Mann whether he believes the rumors surrounding Hitler's death. His response is "Who cares?"[40]

V

"I think we should get back to work," Leo Borchard says over breakfast to his domestic partner, Ruth Andreas-Friedrich, on May 12. "It's time for us to devote ourselves to more useful things than nailing windows shut and cleaning toilets. In any case, I'm going to give my first concert soon." For Ruth, this comes as a bolt out of the blue. She asks, "Concert? Where? And with whom?" She looks at Leo with wide eyes, as if she can't believe her ears. "We'll see," he responds confidently.[41]

Leo Borchard and Ruth Andreas-Friedrich have been a couple since 1931. She's a journalist who has worked for various women's magazines, and he's a respected classical music conductor who has regularly worked with such stellar ensembles as the Berlin Philharmonic and the Orchestre National du France. Ruth has a twenty-year-old daughter named Karin from a previous relationship. Until recently, the three of them existed in a permanent state of high alert, risking their lives every day by helping German Jews. They were joined in their resistance by the writer Fred Denger, the master confectioner Walter Reimann and his wife, Charlotte, the doctors Josef Schunk and Walter Seitz, and a good dozen others. These very diverse men and women formed a network called "Uncle Emil" that supported people persecuted by the Nazi regime, helping them emigrate and procuring food, ration vouchers, and fake identity documents. Group members also tried to alleviate the victims' social suffering by paying them visits.

Leo's offhand announcement that he was ready to give a concert again shakes his friends out of their shock and serves as a sign that the war is truly over. As if they had to convince themselves of that truth, they reassure one another that the Nazis have indeed been driven from power and can't hurt them anymore. The moment is now at hand for the members of "Uncle Emil" to return to their everyday lives. It's May 12, when Leo Borchard decides to put the past behind him. He has only 103 days left to live.

"My little V-E day party was alright," Kurt Weill tells his wife, Lotte Lenya, in a letter from Los Angeles. "We all had dinner here and then went to see the newsreels with the German atrocity pictures—which seems to me a good way of 'celebrating' this victory."[42] The composer hails from Germany, but has lived in the United States for a good ten years, having fled from the Nazis with Lotte. There was a time when Kurt and his librettist, playwright Bertolt Brecht, were celebrities in their homeland. After premiering in Berlin in late August 1928, their work *The Threepenny Opera* became one of the biggest hits in theatrical history. At the height of the Roaring Twenties, Weill and Brecht's songs struck a chord with people everywhere. You couldn't go to a bar without hearing "Mack the Knife" or visit a dance hall without being treated to "Tango Ballad." But then Hitler became German Chancellor.

Kurt was lucky enough to be able to successfully continue his career with Broadway musicals such as *Lady in the Dark* and *One Touch of Venus*. Although he and Lotte live in New City, New York, Kurt often spends several weeks at a time in Los Angeles and occasionally works for the American film industry. At the end of this month, the film *Where Do We Go from Here?*—for which he composed the music—will open. Meanwhile, Lotte sings her husband's songs in New York nightclubs and with a theater company throughout the endless spaces of America.

His fellow emigrants make Kurt uneasy. If he cannot avoid a social occasion with them, he usually keeps it short and sends his "darling" Lotte a detailed report the following day. "I had to go to Slezak's dinner party last night," he carps in August 1944 after visiting the home of actor Walter Slezak. "It was one of the worst gatherings of refugees I've ever gone through. A German language evening of the worst kind—because it wasn't even German but that awful mixture of Hungarian and Viennese." But he did meet writer Franz Werfel and his wife, Alma: "The Werfels were very nice. He is a sick man, and she's an old fool, but strangely warm and cordial to me, and genuinely enthusiastic about *Lady in the Dark*, which she saw twice. A movie and operetta writer, Walter Reisch, was leading the conversation. He ought to be shot right after Hitler."[43]

Kurt has another unwelcome invitation on his schedule in Los Angeles today, May 12. His friend Florence Homolka has asked him to a dinner party at her elegant house in Bel Air. The thirty-four-year-old is the daughter of the wealthy publisher Eugene Meyer and his wife, Agnes, who's considered a confidante of Thomas Mann. In addition to Eugene and the playwright Maxwell Anderson, Thomas and Katia Mann are also expected. Kurt is looking forward to the reunion with the Manns, whom he had only met the previous September—"two very sweet old people, wise, humorous, intelligent, and far superior to all those intellectual refugees of the Brecht crowd."[44] Florence's husband, the Austrian actor Oskar Homolka, has begged off the occasion. Their marriage is on the rocks, and there is already talk of divorce.

That evening, the guests discuss the latest political news from Europe. How could it be otherwise? Thomas Mann is particularly concerned about the situation in Germany, "whose life in the coming decades is hard to imagine." He adds: "For the time being, they will have no schools, no theater, no radio, no newspapers."[45] On this score, Thomas Mann is mistaken. The same Sunday he confided his fears to his diary, the Berlin transport authority put the first bus line back in service, in the Zehlendorf district. That afternoon, Hans von Benda conducts a concert by the Berlin Chamber Orchestra in the public auditorium of the Schöneberg Town Hall, and in the evening, Berlin Radio returns to the air with a one-hour broadcast.

V

Forty-four-year-old Red Army soldier Vasily Petrovich W. writes to his family on May 15: "We are starting to get used to peacetime. It's strange. Our routines proceed strictly according to plan. All sorts of rules, duties, discipline. The Germans have also become more cheerful. They're happy there is no more war. It's been very difficult for them recently. Now they often hang around our kitchen when the soldiers have lunch and leave with a happy smile if they manage to get some leftover soup or bread, which is often the case. Our soldiers have already forgotten their rage and are happy to share with starving Germans. The Germans have already learned to pronounce many words in Russian, first and foremost the words for bread, papirosa, tobacco. Crowds of children in particular follow our soldiers. It's an international gang, and they behave the same everywhere. The smaller ones try to climb into the soldiers' arms; the bigger ones horse around or try to make themselves of use in some way. In general, life has become more monotonous—perhaps a little boring."[46]

V

Down south in Rosenheim, Klaus Mann runs into Curt Riess, an old friend from his carefree youthful years in Berlin. As a Jew, Curt also had to flee Germany in 1933 and now serves in the US Army. Someone told him that great composer Richard Strauss still resides in his villa in Garmisch and receives visitors. A short time ago, a group of American GIs supposedly went to his house, and the musical master played piano for them. Klaus is immediately taken with the idea of visiting Strauss. On the one hand, the aging composer is world famous, and an interview with him would attract Klaus a lot of attention. On the other, Klaus has a score to settle with Strauss, who signed a letter penned by a group of conformist artists denouncing his father Thomas after the Nazis were handed power in 1933. Since then, the Manns have understandably had little good to say about him. Klaus wants to ask Strauss why he signed the denunciation, but he also wants to remain incognito. So off to Garmisch!

Klaus and Curt pose as American reporters to gain access to the composer. "Our conversation took place outside, in the villa's blossoming yard," Klaus would recall, "although of course in much more intimate surroundings than our audience with the Reichsmarshall [Göring]."[47] Strauss is eighty but in good health. There's nothing of an old man about his pink face, his voice is gentle and sonorous, and he speaks with a southern German lilt. What he has to say, however, disappoints his two visitors. The Third Reich was "bothersome" in many respects, he tells them. Klaus and Curt exchange a disbelieving glance. Did he really just use the word "bothersome?" Strauss can read the skepticism in the eyes of the two young men and adds that in the final months of the war, Hitler issued orders that would have allowed people who had been bombed out or driven from their homelands with the advances of the Red Army to be quartered in his villa. He still feels his angry pulse pounding in his temples every time he thinks of that. "Imagine that! Strangers—here in my home!"[48]

"Calm down, Papa," Strauss' daughter-in-law Alice, who is also sitting in the yard, tells him. "It was a terrible idea, an affront, extremely inappropriate, but thank God, it never went beyond an idea. No one ever burdened you with any bombed-out refugees, did they?" But Strauss refuses to be placated. "Of course! Because the war ended!" He asks rhetorically of the group. "But what would have happened had it not? My appeal to Hitler had no effect at all. He insisted that I, too, should make a sacrifice. Quartering refugees! The nerve of it!"[49]

Had he ever considered leaving Nazi Germany, Klaus wants to know. Strauss shakes his head. Why should he have

In late April, US troops take the Bavarian town of Garmisch and set about occupying Richard Strauss's villa, but the composer resists. After the soldiers agree to forgo their plans, a grateful Strauss plays piano for them.

left Germany, he asks back, surprised. "I make my living—a considerable one at that—here... There are at least eighty opera houses in our country."[50] Klaus can't believe his ears. "The naivete with which Strauss admitted to his utterly ruthless, utterly amoral egotism," Klaus will write, "might have been disarming, almost comic, if it weren't an expression of an ethical and intellectual sinkhole."[51] For Thomas Mann's son, Strauss is a "great man—who's utterly without any personal greatness!"[52]

As if that weren't enough, the aged composer tells his visitors that there were a lot of Nazis who were excellent men. Hans Frank, the "Butcher of Poland," for instance, was "very fine, very cultivated—he appreciated my operas." Thanks to former Reich Youth Leader Baldur von Schirach, the Strauss family was given preferential treatment in Vienna, even though his daughter-in-law Alice was a Jew. With visible pride, Strauss proclaims, "I can say that my daughter-in-law was the only free Jewish woman in Germany."[53]

That goes too far even for Alice. "Free? Not really, Papa. At least not entirely." She exhales. "My freedom left much to be desired. You forget what I had to endure. Was I allowed to go hunting? No. For a time, I was even forbidden to ride horses."[54] Klaus can't believe his ears. Millions of people have died because of the Nazis' racist insanity, and Richard Strauss's Jewish daughter-in-law is complaining because she wasn't always allowed to ride and hunt.

At the end of their meeting, Strauss offers his guests an autographed photo. "Thanks, but no thanks," Klaus tells him.

"I'm not a collector."[55] They take their leave. Klaus doesn't know that a few days ago Strauss completed a new composition, "Metamorphoses," for twenty-three solo strings, a profoundly sad elegy for a world in ruins. In this half-hour work, Strauss celebrates musical Romanticism, of which he sees himself as the last representative, he mourns the victims of the war and weeps for the past glory of German art, which in his eyes was so perverted by the "Third Reich." For him, National Socialism is "the most terrible period of humanity," as he notes in these weeks. "A twelve-year reign of bestiality, ignorance, and cultureless stupidity presided over by the greatest criminals."[56] Perhaps Klaus Mann's assessment of the aged Richard Strauss would have been different if he had known about this swan song? Hard to say. Years later, the pianist Glenn Gould would describe the *Metamorphoses* as the most moving musical work of the twentieth century: "Not a day goes by that I don't think of *Metamorphosen*, or hear it in my mind."[57]

Nowhere during his travels through Germany does Klaus Mann encounter any "true" Nazis. For Germans, National Socialism was at most "bothersome," to use Strauss's term, and naturally no one knew a thing about the horrible crimes committed in their names. "Suddenly they all were discovering their democratic pasts and, if possible, their 'non-Aryan' grandma," Klaus writes to a friend. "Jewish relatives are in great demand."[58] Surely somewhere between Kiel and Garmisch there must be someone willing to own up to the past. The search goes on.

After the war, large parts of Europe lie in ruins. Persons unknown identify the guilty party on a building exterior on Pfalzburger Straße in the Berlin district of Wilmersdorf. The words read: "It took Hitler 12 years to do this."

V

"Are the Americans coming or not?" Ruth Andreas-Friedrich asks in mid-May. "Will Berlin be divided or left to the Russians? So many questions, so many opinions."[59] The most pressing problem, however, is the catastrophic disruption of supplies for the civilian population. On the same Tuesday that Richard Strauss engages in his musings in Garmisch, a decree comes into force in Berlin to ensure the daily distribution of food. The citizens of the city are divided into four groups. Heavy laborers and those who work in dangerous conditions, for example, receive 600 grams of bread and 100 grams of meat. Normal workers get 500 grams of bread and 65 grams of meat, while white-collar workers are allowed 400 grams of bread and 40 grams of meat. Children, nonworking family members, and the rest of the population have to make do with just 300 grams of bread and 20 grams of meat. Their ration cards are popularly known as "cemetery cards" since they entitle bearers to only slightly more than 1,200 calories a day—too little to live on but just enough to keep them from dying.

"Can you buy anything with it?" asks Ruth's daughter Karin when she holds her ration card in her hands for the first time. "Try it out," a friend advises. When she returns to the apartment a few hours later, Karin has three pounds of groats and half a kilo of rock salt in her shopping net. No bread, meat, sugar, or fat. "The rest will come later," she explains to her perplexed mother. "Transportation problems! Because of the bridges."[60]

V

Red Army soldier Mikhail A. B., who was born in Tashkent in 1921, writes to his family on May 20: "I am scribbling these lines in the Reichstag, from whose dome the red banner of victory is flying. I've driven around all over the city, been to Hitler's private chamber, visited the ruins of Goebbels' house and been to the famous Brandenburg Gate, to various monuments. Berlin now lies on its knees before us."[61]

V

"A newspaper is now being published, although naturally it's difficult to get hold of," Else Tietze notes in her diary on the Monday after Pentecost. "The decrees all sound fine and dandy. But the atrocities that the Nazis are supposed to have committed make your heart stand still. If only a small part is true, it's more than enough."[62] The date is May 21. There is still no trace of her family.

V

There are days when Thomas Selvester terribly misses his Scottish home with its highlands, glittering lochs, and dense forests. He longs for the city of his birth, Edinburgh, its castle perched majestically on volcanic rock, where Mary Queen of Scots, also known as Mary Stuart, once lived and where her son, the future King James VI, was born in June 1566. Founded in 843 CE, the small German city of Lüneburg around fifty kilometers southeast of Hamburg is almost as old as Edinburgh. Tom, as his friends call him, is deployed as a captain in a British interrogation camp there. One of his jobs is to filter Nazi war criminals from the columns of refugees and homeless people wandering through the country. That's easier said than done. Around eighteen thousand displaced persons from East and West Prussia, Posen, Pomerania, and Silesia have found shelter in Lüneburg alone, which normally has a population of just under forty thousand. There are also as many as thirty thousand victims of Nazi persecution and deportation—mainly liberated concentration camp prisoners, forced laborers, and prisoners of war—waiting to return to their home countries. It is easy for someone to disappear in this vast multitude.

On Wednesday, May 23, another truck full of potentially suspicious people arrives at the Lüneburg interrogation camp, including three Germans who had been picked up two days previously by British soldiers on a bridge near Bremervörde, around 110 kilometers to the west. Tom initially pays no attention to the new arrivals, but when one of the men insists on seeing the officer in charge, Tom has the trio brought to him. "The first man to enter my office was small, ill-looking and shabbily dressed, but he was immediately followed by two other men, both of whom were tall and soldierly looking, one slim and one well-built" he later recalled.[63] The small man, who is wearing a patch over his left eye, is carrying papers made out in the name of Heinrich Hitzinger. He asks if he can speak to Tom. Tom nods and gives the order to take the two others out of the room. Then the man takes off his eye patch, puts on a pair of glasses with round lenses and identifies himself in a low, flat voice as Heinrich Himmler.

Tom is thunderstruck, but he quickly pulls himself together and informs the Second Army's headquarters. A Major Rice, a secret service staff officer, arrives at the camp at around 7:30 p.m. to confirm Himmler's identity. And indeed, sitting in front of them is the dreaded "Reichsführer SS" and head of the German police, the Reich Minister of the Interior and the commander of the reserve army—to name but a few of Himmler's offices—and one of the most heinous mass murderers of all time.

Major Rice orders the man searched immediately, which Tom and his sergeant do personally. It is widely known that Nazis often carry lethal poison with them, to kill themselves and evade arrest, and Himmler has to be held accountable at all costs. "In his jacket I found a small brass case, similar to a cartridge case, which contained a small glass phial. I recognized it for what it was, but asked Himmler what it contained, and he said: 'That is my medicine. It cures stomach cramp.' I also found a similar brass case, but without the phial, and came to the conclusion that the phial was hidden somewhere on the prisoner's person."

Tom has Himmler patted down once again, thoroughly, but no trace of the vial is found. Finally, he sends for thick cheese sandwiches and tea, which he offers to Himmler. If the vial was in his mouth, he calculated, Himmler would have to remove it before eating. Tom: "I watched him closely, whilst he was eating, but did not notice anything unusual."

Late that evening, Heinrich Himmler is transferred to the headquarters of the security forces on Uelzener Strasse 31a. At 11:00 p.m., in a bay window room on the first floor of the three-story brick villa, military doctor C. J. Wells examines the prisoner again. Colonel Michael Murphy from the Secret Service, Major Norman Whittaker, and Company Sergeant Major Edwin Austin are also present.

Himmler has to undress completely and now stands naked in front of Wells. The doctor orders the windows closed and puts a blanket over Himmler's shoulders. The procedure is carried out without incident. Himmler is suspicious but cooperative. "I noticed that his fingernails were cut to a point which in a man I had always coupled, probably quite wrongly, with a sex perversion," Wells would recall. Wells tells Himmler to open his mouth and looks in at his teeth. "They were goodish teeth with a certain number of gold fillings and some small round amalgam ones in the fissures of his molars."[64] But what is this small, blue object stuck in a crease of his left cheek? When Wells asks him to come closer to the lamp, Himmler bites down on the tiny capsule hidden there. His face turns deep red and contorts in pain. "We immediately upended the old bastard and got his mouth into the bowl of water which was there to wash the poison out," Major Whittaker will confide to his diary.[65] "There were terrible groans and grunts coming from the swine." Himmler's tongue was hastily fixed with a needle and thread to prevent him from swallowing the poison whole. "The stench coming from Himmler's mouth was unmistakably that of hydrocyanic, and the dose must have been enough to kill an elephant," Dr. Wells will remember.[66] After a quarter of an hour, he stops the resuscitation attempts: "It was a losing battle, and this evil thing breathed its last at 23:14."[67]

"Tomorrow at ten a.m. is my first rehearsal," Leo Borchard tells Ruth Andreas-Friedrich on May 24.[68] She can't believe her ears. It's less than a month since the fighting in Berlin ended, and Leo is rehearsing a concert with the Berlin Philharmonic. Borchard has done the impossible. Riding his rickety bicycle through the city, he's drummed up the various orchestra musicians, gotten hold of instruments and sheet music, and procured the necessary permissions. But what will be the venue? The Philharmonic on Bernburger Strasse was destroyed in January 1944. "On the spot where Bruno

Walter once made music, between rubble and remnants of walls, lies a dead white horse," Ruth will recall, "its body bloated, its eyes black and stony."[69] But Leo and his fellow musicians quickly find a solution. The Titania Palast, a huge cinema that opened in 1928 in the southern Berlin neighborhood of Steglitz, suffered only slight damage during the war. It has a sufficiently large stage and room for an audience of at least 1,900 people. The first postwar performance by the Berlin Philharmonic will take place there on May 26. That day at 5:00 p.m., Leo mounts his bike, pins his trouser legs, and sets off. Ruth, Karin, and other friends follow, on cycles as well. There is already a large crowd before the entrance of the Titania Palast waiting for admission. These people have come from everywhere in the city to Steglitz, many by bike, others on foot, to hear the Philharmonic. The concert sells out in no time.

Leo stands backstage and struggles with his tie, shifting his weight nervously from one foot to the other. In a few minutes, he'll give his musicians their cue and make history. Although Leo has performed quite often in Berlin, concerts here remain special occasions. Berlin audiences are as demanding as they are critical, known for giving musicians a difficult time. Many a world-famous virtuoso, unacquainted with the local habits, has been left scratching his head at the lack of response elicited from his listeners.

Leo and his musicians have come up with a clever program for the evening. They start with the overture to *Ein Sommernachtstraum* (*A Midsummer Night's Dream*) by

Felix Mendelssohn-Bartholdy, whose works were banned in the Third Reich. That's followed by a Mozart violin concerto and, in a nod to the Soviet authorities in control of Berlin, Tchaikovsky's Fourth Symphony.

A deeply pitched gong sounds, and the attendants open the door. Leo tugs one last time at his tie and takes the director's podium. Many people in the audience shut their eyes to listen more intensely to Mendelssohn's music, which has not been heard in Germany for the past twelve years. After a few minutes of reverie, the doors to the cinema suddenly fly open, and a handful of Soviet officers march loudly to the seats reserved for them. A few members of the audience turn around with the fingers on their lips to hush the late arrivals, but when they see the soldiers with their machine guns, they quickly desist. Leo doesn't allow himself to be distracted and keeps on conducting. During the final movement of the Tchaikovsky, the officers get up and leave. The audience can enjoy the concert's final minutes without disruption. "Conductor Leo Borchard demonstrated his complete mastery," the newly founded *Tagesspiegel* newspaper will write three days later. "The orchestra was unquestionably at the peak of its musical ability."[70]

Late that evening, Leo and Ruth repair to their balcony. Neither can sleep after his triumphant concert. Too many thoughts buzz around in their heads, and they are too deeply moved. Leo lights a cigarette and takes a deep drag. Lost in his thoughts, he looks up at the stars, as he slowly releases the smoke into the mild air. "The fact that we've been allowed to live, that we've survived...," he tells his lover in a soft voice.[71] He doesn't finish his sentence. Leo Borchard has ninety days to live.

Else Tietze is furious. "The day before yesterday, I felt terrible rage and wished I could counteract the lies in the *Berliner Zeitung*," she complains to her diary on May 28. "'No more lining up,' Berliners are being supplied with plenty of food. 'The Berlin population is breathing a sigh of relief' and so on. Yet on Saturday, starting at 6:00 a.m., there were lines, the likes of which I have never seen, in front of all the grocery stores. Word was that there would finally be butter, which we've been longing for. A few people got some very early, but then no more was put on sale. The crowd was instructed to wait, and later they were told that they had received three-quarter pounds of meat (the famous 'Stalin donation'). As a result, workers could claim a small fraction of their fat allowance, and the 'remaining ones' none at all, and only ninety grams of meat (people doing physical labor got a little more). Most people had been standing in line for hours."[72]

Mrs. Tietz has had no word from her family.

"I am profoundly concerned about the European situation," writes Prime Minister Churchill to President Truman.

Although victory over Germany has been achieved, peace is still a long way off, with the war against Japan continuing with undiminished ferocity. Troops previously stationed in Europe will soon have to be transferred to the Pacific. "Meanwhile what is to happen about Russia?" he asks the American president. Churchill is disillusioned by Stalin's crass power politics in the eastern part of Central Europe. He distrusts the Soviets who are clearly doing everything they can to install puppet regimes in the territories occupied by the Red Army. "An iron curtain is drawn down upon their front," the prime minister continues. "We do not know what is going on behind. There seems little doubt that the whole of the regions east of the line Lübeck-Trieste-Corfu will soon be completely in their hands." What could a joint policy toward Germany look like under these circumstances? Germany needs help, the prime minister states. Otherwise, millions will starve to death next winter. And what should be done with the war criminals being apprehended everywhere? There's no end to the unresolved questions. "Surely it is vital now to come to an understanding with Russia, or see where we are with her, before we weaken our Armies mortally or retire to the zones of occupation. This can only be done by a personal meeting."[73]

Truman and Stalin agree in principle to Churchill's wish for a joint postwar conference, but there is disagreement about the timing. Churchill would prefer to meet as soon as possible, but Truman refuses, citing his obligations in Washington.

Stalin is in no hurry. The longer the date can be delayed, he reasons, the more time he'll have to create a fait accompli in Eastern Europe. After some back and forth, the parties agree on July 15 as a date. France, it is also agreed, won't be invited. Although the country had been granted its own occupation zone at the Yalta Conference in February, there have been difficulties with the head of the provisional Parisian government. Charles de Gaulle is being more quarrelsome than ever in Churchill's eyes, making France an unreliable partner. Although Truman doesn't share his predecessor Roosevelt's contempt for de Gaulle, he doesn't want the unpredictable general at the table either. Stalin, for his part, considers France to be nothing more than an insignificant regional power.

The question of a suitable venue remains. Truman half-heartedly suggests a location in Alaska, while Churchill favors an undestroyed city in West Germany. But Stalin says "nyet" to both ideas. For him, Berlin is the only option. "I shall be very glad," Churchill finally wired the Soviet leader on May 29 with a characteristic touch of black humor, "to meet you and President Truman in what is left of Berlin."[74]

V

The Berliner Rundfunk radio station now broadcasts daily from 6:00 a.m. to 1:00 a.m. May 29 begins with the news, followed by early-morning gymnastics. After the half-hour program "Zwischen Tau und Tag" (Between dew and day),

Necessity is the mother of invention. Little more than the outer walls of this building remain standing, but a woman has set up a makeshift home in her bombed-out apartment. The potted plants are an essential component.

there is another early morning gymnastics session, followed by more news and "Gymnastics for Women." Throughout the day, there are various musical performances interspersed with talk shows. In the afternoon, there is a "program for housewives," followed by music by Beethoven and Tchaikovsky. In the evening, there's dance music although programmers are desperately searching for "records and sheet music of music not previously played on the radio," as one newspaper advertisement euphemistically puts it.[75] Jewish composers such as Giacomo Meyerbeer, Felix Mendelssohn Bartholdy, Emmerich Kálmán, and Paul Abraham were banned during the Third Reich, and anyone in possession of scores or recordings should contact the station.

On the morning of May 30, Else Tietze leaves her apartment and sets off on an adventure. At least that's how she feels walking the ten kilometers from the Steglitz neighborhood to the former government district in Mitte to visit her friends, the Zanders, whose last registered address was on Wilhelmstrasse. In addition to a jam sandwich and a thermos flask of tea, she carries a map of Berlin in her handbag to help her find her way through the ruins. Is the Zanders' house still standing? Are they even still alive? Else has no idea.

At Papestrasse train station, Else briefly strays from her route, but after a few hundred meters of accidentally walking across the tracks, she knows where she is again. At

Hallesches Tor square, she hunkers down on a block of stone to rest for a while. Her feet hurt. She eats her jam sandwich and drinks a cup of tea, then continues on. It's not far to the government district now. With every step she takes north along Wilhelmstrasse, her unease grows. Wherever Else looks, there is nothing but piles of rubble. The once magnificent boulevard with its wide sidewalks, elegant villas and palaces, prestigious government buildings, and cultivated gardens and parks has ceased to exist. "It's simply impossible to imagine that this part of Berlin can be rebuilt," she writes in her diary. "If only we could have shown Hitler and his ilk what they did here!"[76]

By some miracle, the Zanders' house has survived the war. Else climbs the stairs, treading heavily, but when she knocks on the door, a young man she doesn't know opens. He says he's a lodger. Mr. and Mrs. Zander are not in, he explains, but he will be happy to give them Else's regards. Else makes her way home, mission unaccomplished. On the way, she encounters horse carts full of refugees from somewhere going somewhere else. Those on the carts look exhausted, while others pull handcarts behind them. For a brief moment, Else feels fortunate. But then her judgmental side reemerges. "One of the things that upset me the most were the women walking with the Russian soldiers and giving them looks—I wanted to slap them in the face," she writes. "Do these creatures have no feeling at all (to say nothing of patriotism) in their bodies? Their kind should be publicly flogged."[77]

V

During the month of May 1945, 977 men and women commit suicide in Berlin, the former capital of the Third Reich. The previous month, it was 3,881 people, including Adolf and Eva Hitler, née Braun.[78]

In the summer of 1945 cultural life slowly resumes in Berlin. Here posters are being pasted up advertising the reopening of the Staatsoper opera house.

FRIENDS AND ENEMIES

Where can he be? Willi Schaeffers shifts uneasily from one foot to the other, fiddling with his bow tie. He repeatedly checks his golden pocket watch, glancing at the dial and shaking his head in confusion. He's nervous. In just a few minutes, his new revue, *Roses Scattered on the Path,* is set to premiere. But where is Heino Gaze? The show can't start without the musical director.

Until last summer, when the war forced it to close, the sixty-year-old Schaeffers ran Berlin's famous "Cabaret of Comedians." Today, on June 1, 1945, he plans to reopen it at Café Leon in Lehniner Platz. He's managed to gather a number of well-known performers such as Evelyn Künneke, Hilde Seipp, Alfred Beierle, and Georg Thomalla. As always, he'll be the master of ceremonies. Schaeffers is a talented emcee who knows how to win over an audience in a casual, seemingly inoffensive way. But his jokes aren't really innocent. Schaeffers specializes in double entendres, something that put him repeatedly at odds multiple times during the Nazi years with the Nazis' prudish propaganda minister, Joseph Goebbels.

Gaze finally arrives, over an hour late, with an unusual excuse. On his way to the theater, Soviet soldiers stopped him and made him help dig up unexploded bombs—even though he was wearing a tuxedo. Gaze quickly brushes the dust off his clothes, then the curtain rises.

"Every performance was sold out," Schaeffers will later recall. "Crowds of poor, frightened people, who could finally relax in the knowledge that it was all over, turned out in droves."[1] Clearly, his brand of humor strikes a chord. In one skit, someone reads a long-winded decree in Russian, whereupon Schaeffers quips, absurdly, "It's equally clear in German."[2] The undisputed star of the evening is thirty-five-year-old soubrette Brigitte Mira. Gaze has composed a song for her, which she sings at the end of the revue in an innocent voice:

My heart feels completely beat
as I walk down the street
You don't have to be from Berlin
to know what it is I'm thinkin'!

But what's the point of feeling glum
After all, what's done is done

And despite it all, deep within
I still believe in Berlin!

Berlin will come back
So goes the song we're all singing
And now across the entire city
So beautifully that song is ringing.

With this little ditty, Gaze has composed the soundtrack to this summer. The song captures the Berlin populace's unbreakable will to survive just four weeks after the fall of the Third Reich. "The audience clapped, laughed, cheered and cried all at once," Mira will remember. "It was a grotesque situation—to sing such a song, so shortly after the war, amidst the ruins of a city that had once been a metropolis."[3]

Klaus Mann and Curt Riess finally succeed in their search for someone in Germany who will admit to being a Nazi. In Oberwarmensteinach, a sleepy village in the Fichtelgebirge mountains, lives a woman who was close friends with Hitler. Rumor has it that the two even had a brief affair, though this is likely just gossip. She bears a name Klaus Mann's father, Thomas, holds in the highest esteem. Winifred Wagner is the daughter-in-law of Richard Wagner, the Führer's favorite composer. Klaus and Curt are well aware of the photos showing Winifred and Hitler in close conversation: Winifred, a "horsey type," in a flowing gown, Hitler in a tuxedo. For years, Hitler regularly attended the Bayreuth Festival and stayed with the Wagners. Klaus reasons that if anyone knows Hitler well, it must be Winifred Wagner. After Villa Wahnfried, the Wagners' Bayreuth ancestral home, was destroyed in the war, Winifred retreated to her vacation home in Oberwarmensteinach, around thirty kilometers away. The forty-seven-year-old awaits her visitors there on June 2.

When Winifred realizes that the two GIs speak fluent German and are obviously of German origin, she immediately switches to English, which she, as a native Englishwoman, speaks perfectly. She makes a joke of it, quickly realizing that the English of the two "supposed Americans" isn't exactly flawless.[4] For Winifred, this is more than a prank. She fundamentally despises men like Klaus Mann and Curt Riess, who, as she sees it, have stabbed their homeland in the back. If they are going to turn up at her house in American uniforms, they should at least speak English.

Curt is so intimidated by the maneuver that he falls into an awkward silence, leaving Klaus to bring up her relationship with Hitler. "Were we friends?" Winifred repeats incredulously. "Of course, we were! Certainly! And how!" Klaus tacitly hoped for a frank admission of this kind: "She seemed to be still proud of it all! Head held high, voluptuous and blonde, she sat opposite me, a Valkyrie of imposing stature and imposing impudence." Winifred makes no bones about her views when she says of Hitler: "He was charming.

I don't know much about politics, but I know a lot about men. Hitler was charming. A real Austrian, you know! Comfortable and cozy! And his sense of humor was simply wonderful." Later, looking back on the conversation, Klaus will note that Winifred was the only person "who had the courage, or at least the imposing cheek, to stand up for Hitler."[5]

V

"Recently, I was a bit taken aback at how much I'd written," Else Tietze confides in her diary on June 4. "Is there any point? When will anyone ever read these scribblings?"[6] She still has heard nothing from her family.

V

"They lived pretty well, the parasites," says a young Red Army soldier, guarding a villa, to the Russian-British journalist Alexander Werth. The man, perhaps nineteen or twenty, is wearing a bronze medal on his chest that reads "For the Defense of Stalingrad." He's clearly been through hell and somehow survived, and now he stands in the picturesque, lakeside neighborhood of Wendenschloss in the district of Köpenick, watching over a historic building that used to belong to some rich German. Werth has never heard of "Wendenschloss." It doesn't really feel like Berlin, he thinks, as the soldier continues to rail against the Germans. There is little in this part of Berlin of the devastation that the war brought to the Reich capital. Around the villa, jasmine is in full bloom, its intense, honey-like, floral scent wafting through the streets. Birds chirp in the trees and the blue waters of the Long Lake shimmer at the end of a tranquil avenue. "Yes, they lived well, the parasites," the soldier repeats, looking disparagingly at the villa. "Great big farms in East Prussia, and pretty posh houses in the towns that hadn't been burned out or bombed to hell. And look at these dachas here! Why did these people who were living so well have to invade us!"[7]

Werth shrugs his shoulders and looks disinterested. He is here for other reasons than to chat with a soldier about the Germans' houses. The forty-four-year-old originally comes from St. Petersburg but fled with his family to Great Britain to escape the turmoil of the October Revolution in 1917. He now works as a journalist for the BBC, among other outlets. Someone has told him that today history will be made here in the southeastern corner of Berlin.

It is Tuesday, June 5, at 5:00 p.m., when the commanders-in-chief of the American, British, Soviet, and French armed forces meet in a former restaurant on Niebergallstraße 20 in Wendenschloss. Since the Wehrmacht's surrender at the beginning of May, the Soviet military administration has governed not just the Soviet occupation zone but all of Berlin. Now, "in view of Germany's defeat," a declaration is to be signed that will officially grant the four victorious powers supreme governmental power. That document requires

Germany, whatever that may entail at this point, to submit to "all demands that may be imposed on it now or later," although there is no talk of Germany being "annexed."[8] The Berlin Declaration, as the document is christened, also contains further agreements, for instance, the establishment of an Allied Control Council, which will decide on all matters concerning Germany as a whole. Last but not least, the German territory of 1937 will be split into occupation zones and Berlin divided into four sectors.

But there's a difference between words and reality, and only time will tell what the latter will turn out to be. It's already evident to Werth and the other journalists that the cooperation between the four powers is unlikely to be free of tension. Marshal Georgy Zhukov makes his colleagues General Dwight D. Eisenhower, Field Marshal Bernard L. Montgomery, and General Jean de Lattre de Tassigny wait a good five hours before he begins the ceremony. Once the documents have been signed—the actual ceremony only takes a few minutes—Zhukov invites them to dinner. The table is richly laid with caviar, smoked salmon, fish, and cold cuts, with several bottles of wine and vodka in front of each plate. It appears a feast is in the offing, with countless speeches and toasts, but Eisenhower is not playing along. The commander-in-chief of the American occupying forces cannot be kept waiting for hours with impunity. Because of the long delay to the start of meeting, he says, his time is now running short, and he unfortunately cannot stay any longer, whereupon he and his delegation march out of the room. "I am sure," General Lucius D. Clay will remember, "the Russians did not expect him to leave on schedule and that it proved an effective lesson."[9]

By chance, on the fringes of the conference, Werth meets Vasily Sokolovsky, whom he had already occasionally encountered in previous years as a war reporter. Hitler's death, the Red Army General admits with a smile on his face, fills him with satisfaction. But when Werth asks him about the behavior of the Soviet troops in Germany, Sokolowski reacts irritably. "Of course, a lot of nasty things happened," he says. "But what do you expect? You know what the Germans did to their Russian war prisoners, how they devastated our country, how they murdered and raped and looted. Have you seen Maidanek or Auschwitz? Every one of our soldiers lost dozens of his comrades. Every one of them had some personal scores to settle with the Germans, and in the first flush of victory our fellows no doubt derived a certain satisfaction from making it hot for those Herrenvolk women. However, that stage is over. We have now pretty well clamped down on that sort of thing—not that most German women are vestal virgins. Our main worry," he grinned, "is the awful spread of the clap among our troops."[10]

On June 6, Thomas Mann turns seventy. The occasion is more than just a milestone birthday for one of many

German-speaking writers living in sunny California, whose numbers also include Lion Feuchtwanger, Franz Werfel, Gina Kaus, and Thomas's brother Heinrich Mann. But most Americans likely aren't aware of when those authors have their birthdays. Thomas Mann is unique in that he represents not just German literature but the good, free, antifascist Germany itself—the real German nation. At least that's how he sees himself. When the Nobel laureate arrived in the United States in February 1938, he dictated a statement to journalists that left no doubt about his self-appointed status: "Wherever I am, Germany is."[11]

A short time later, Thomas Mann embarked on a major lecture tour across the New World. In Salt Lake City, a local newspaper dubbed him as "Hitler's most intimate enemy,"[12] and in Boston, demand for tickets was so great that more than a thousand people had to be turned away. By 1943, Mann had completed four more tours, reaching hundreds of thousands of Americans. Interviews and social invitations followed every lecture, further boosting his fame. Americans regard Mann as "the Greatest Living Man of Letters," as posters and newspaper ads proclaimed, although, as he wrote a friend in 1943, there was something "confusing and incomprehensible" about it all. "I ask myself all the time: What do these people expect? After all, I'm not Caruso!"[13]

But there's nothing he can do about that. Wherever Thomas Mann is, free Germany is, so it's no wonder that the celebrations for Hitler's intimate enemy's seventieth birthday turn into a party lasting several weeks. Ahead of the

A crowd is drawn in Berlin in May 1945, as the first postwar newspaper is distributed.

festivities there is a commemorative publication, conceived by Mann's publisher Gottfried Bermann Fischer, with a list of authors reading like a who's who of German literature. Franz Werfel, Arnold Zweig, Hermann Hesse, Annette Kolb, Carl Zuckmayer, and Heinrich Mann are among those who pay tribute to the Nobel prizewinner. Then a triumphal tour through the United States begins.

After a brief stay in Chicago, Thomas Mann and his wife, Katia, arrive in Washington DC on May 28, where they attend a breakfast at the home of his patron Agnes E. Meyer. Agnes comes from a German immigrant family and is married to the wealthy entrepreneur and owner of the *Washington Post*, Eugene Meyer. The Meyers have excellent connections to America's cultural and political elite and live in a feudal forty-room mansion on Crescent Place and an equally expansive country house of no fewer than 2,600 square meters in Mount Kisco, north of New York City. It was Mrs. Meyer who gave Thomas Mann an honorary position as "Consultant in Germanic Literature" at the Library of Congress in 1941, which sounds like more work than it is. His main obligation is to spend two weeks a year in the capital and give a lecture. In return, he receives a handsome salary of $4,800, roughly what a university professor makes in a year. It's paid by Mrs. Meyer.

The next day, May 29, Mann gives his annual speech in the Library of Congress—this time on "Germany and the Germans"—and in the evening Agnes and Eugene Meyer host a reception with seventy guests for their friend. But not everything about his stay at his wealthy hosts' house is to the writer's liking. On one occasion, he complains in his diary about the host ("Dinner with Eugene, increasingly boring and sleepy"), another time about the meager meals he was served.[14] Imagine that!

Mann's next stop, on June 6, is New York itself, where he celebrates his birthday. In the salon of his suite in the St. Regis Hotel on the corner of Fifth Avenue and 55th Street, the tables groan under the mass of flowers and congratulatory missives. But that's not all. American high society wants to get a closer look at the famous writer, and he and Katia are shuttled from one party to another. A curious incident occurs at one festive reception, when Zuckmayer, having already downed a few too many drinks, asks to speak. He will now recite his poem "Cognac in Spring" in honor of his esteemed colleague, he slurs, while accompanying himself on the lute. "Zuck," as he is called by his friends, stamps both feet, plucks wildly at the strings and warbles "I drowned in the brown cognac lake..." in a piercing voice. This bizarre birthday serenade arouses the "displeasure of the jubilarian, who was very averse to such excesses and had difficulty maintaining a positive demeanor," as one guest will recall.[15]

Thomas Mann has put an exhausting few weeks behind him on June 20 when he and Katia embark on their return journey to Los Angeles. The train trip drags on and on, and the author also has some complaints about the waiting times in the dining car. "Had to line up from eight-thirty to about nine for breakfast," carps Mann in his diary. "Silly, shameful and outrageous. Only Americans can maintain a good mood and appetite in such a situation."[16]

V

"Writing is getting harder and harder because my heart is getting heavier and heavier. My dear, dear children! Sometimes I think I can't do it anymore." It's Friday, June 8, and Else Tietze is completely desperate. There has been no sign of life from her offspring for more than two months now. "There is no prospect of hearing from you or seeing you again in the foreseeable future. If only you are healthy and not starving. All we do here is stand in line. We've each been given a number. Maybe that will help, but you always have to watch out for when and if anything's available. Four times now, we've been fobbed off at the butcher's with 'probably tomorrow.' I don't really care, but naturally you take what little you can get."[17]

V

The Red Army soldier Andrey Andreyevich U. from Tarnogski Gorodok near Vologda in northwest Russia writes to his wife, Musja, on June 8: "I was in the Reichstag. I climbed to the top of the ruins of the building. The whole thing, from the entrance to the uppermost groups of sculpture under the ceiling in the main auditorium, is covered with visitors' scribbled hometowns: Moscow, Saratov, Tbilisi, and all the other cities, but I didn't see Vologda. I climbed to the top and wrote 'Vologda' on the ledge. You can even see it from below, from the square, even from the Brandenburg Gate. I also wrote 'Kokschenga—Berlin,' 'Tarnogski Gorodok—Berlin.' I didn't march more than 3,000 kilometers for nothing!"[18]

V

The German POW Alfred Misselhorn has been transferred from the transit camp in Bretzenheim to the French city of Rennes in Brittany. Here he's interned in a camp named after the French politician Léon Gambetta. After France lost the Franco-Prussian war of 1870–71, Gambetta was one of the founding fathers of the "Third Republic" and a vehement advocate of revanchism toward Germany. "Toujours y penser, jamais en parler" was his motto—"Always think but never talk of it!"

On June 9, Alfred Misselhorn stands in the camp courtyard stripped to the waist and with his hands over his head. "They're looking for members of the Waffen SS," he later notes in his journal. "They have the blood type tattooed under their arm. Many are also said to have tried to remove the tattoo by cutting it out, so those men with corresponding scars are identified and taken away. We stay in the courtyard until those men have left the camp. We are then shown a photographic documentation of the crimes committed in the concentration camps. We see mountains of dead bodies and large pictures of those camp inmates who managed to stay alive. Horrible images, our spirits sink, but do we actually look that much better?"[19]

For the time being, the camp is being run by the Americans, but rumors are growing that the French could soon take over sole command. Alfred is afraid. What is to become of him, one of the adolescents who until recently were the Führer's last hope?

V

On June 13, passersby discover a male corpse in the Berlin district of Karlshorst. The body is found in an abandoned signalman's hut on the Prussian Eastern Railway line from Berlin via Königsberg to Eydtkuhnen on the Lithuanian border. Detective Inspector Gustav Durnio has a hard time getting to the scene of the crime, losing his way several times on railroad property, but eventually reaching his goal. There he sees a scene of devastation. The hut's ceiling is caved in, its doors and windows are missing, and the floor is littered with rubble and garbage. A dead man lies in the middle of this mess, his body badly mauled and displaying numerous external injuries. Durnio bends over the body and searches his clothes for personal papers such as an ID card, a letter, or a soldier's log. Nothing. But next to the body he finds a soaked photo and a piece of paper on which something is written in Cyrillic. The detective inspector reaches into his jacket pocket and pulls out a magnifying glass to examine the faded photograph. Gustav Durnio immediately recognizes a man in uniform. Perhaps it's the deceased. But a detail attracts his suspicion. It's difficult to make out, so he squints with his left eye. After a few seconds, Durnio lifts his head and puts the magnifying glass back in its case. He's deciphered what he was looking at. The man in the photo was wearing an SS uniform.[20]

When sixty-one-year-old Olga Maria Theresia Gustava Sternheim—Thea for short—looks back on her life thus far, it almost makes her dizzy. All the ups and downs! She used to live in a veritable palace in Pullach near Munich, but today she has to make do with a modest studio in Rue Antoine Chantin in Paris's 14th arrondissement. The brilliant triumphs and bitter disappointments! She married her first husband, Arthur Löwenstein, on the sly and against the wishes of her Catholic parents. Their union did not last long. Her relationship with her second husband, the playwright Carl Sternheim, with whom she led a life of luxury thanks to an inheritance, also failed. After ten years, they divorced, and in 1927 Thea settled in Berlin, where her daughter Dorothea—Mopsa, as everyone called her—was living.

Born in 1905, Mopsa Sternheim was part of the *jeunesse*

dorée around the siblings Klaus and Erika Mann. The illustrated magazines of the German capital regularly reported on the latest escapades of these spoiled children of literary giants, and more than one notable writer, including Kurt Tucholsky in his magazine *Die Weltbühne*, also poked fun at them. In addition to Mopsa, Klaus, and Erika, and Carl Sternheim's son from his first marriage, Carlhans, the clique also included Gerhart Hauptmann's son, Benvenuto, and Mopsa's best friend, Pamela Wedekind, who was engaged to Klaus for four years before marrying Mopsa's father, Carl Sternheim. Tucholsky mocked them with consummate malice:

> "We hear that Benvenuto Hauptmann has become engaged to Klaus Mann. As is customary in such cases, the wedding will take place on the hoity-toity island Hiddensee.
>
> Pamela Wedekind, Erika Mann and Mops Sternheim will be performing in a "Review by four" next Tuesday. Their parents have rushed to Berlin from Austria and Munich—and been moved, no doubt, by a flood of parental pride.
>
> We hear that Klaus Mann has begun a two-volume novel and a collection of travel aphorisms. It is feared that the novel will be published at the end of this year.
>
> Benvenuto Hauptmann has divorced Klaus Mann because before the marriage he was not aware of his bride's normal tendencies.
>
> Carlhans Sternheim and siblings Klaus Mann and Pamela Wedekind have set off on a journey around the world

> with their sister-in-law Erika Mann to get Rabindranath Tagore to finally sort out their tangled family relationships.
>
> Klaus Mann has sprained his right arm composing his hundredth advertising slogan and will be unable to speak for the next few weeks."[21]

The young people's wild, luxurious, exuberant, sensual lifestyle came to an abrupt end. Thea Sternheim sensed the danger posed by the up-and-coming Nazi party early on. If Hitler came to power, which she believed was only a matter of time, she no longer wanted to remain in Germany. She moved to Paris in early 1932, with Mopsa following a year later.

Mother and daughter managed to get by, but in early December 1943 Mopsa, who was active in the French Resistance, was arrested by the Gestapo and deported two months later with 958 French women to the Ravensbrück women's concentration camp.

It is only now, in June 1945, that Thea Sternheim learns her daughter has survived. Mopsa was lucky enough to be one of around seven thousand women rescued by the Swedish Red Cross from the completely overcrowded camp shortly before the end of the war and brought to safety in Sweden. Since Mopsa's arrest a year and almost seven months ago, not a day has gone by that Thea hasn't thought of her. How often has she imagined a knock at the door of her studio and Mopsa standing in the doorway? When will mother and daughter be able to embrace again?

V

While Thea Sternheim waits for her daughter to return, an august military ceremony takes place at the Arc de Triomphe, about six kilometers from Rue Antoine Chantin. It's Thursday, June 14, and Charles de Gaulle is awarding the Ordre de la Libération to General Dwight D. Eisenhower, commander-in-chief of the Allied forces in northwestern Europe. It's the third major accolade "Ike"—who, like de Gaulle, was born in 1890—has received in a week. Just two days earlier, he had been made an honorary citizen ("Freedom of the City") in London and decorated with the Order of Merit.

"Patriam servando victoriam tulit" reads the small square bronze medal de Gaulle pins on the left of his guest of honor's chest: "By serving the country, he helped it to victory." The honor is for Eisenhower's service in the liberation of France. "The Corps Diplomatique were, as usual, very badly placed at this ceremony," British ambassador Duff Cooper complains later in his diary. "I sometimes think de Gaulle may go mad. He looked awful today from what I could see of him at the Arc de Triomphe, where he conferred the Cross of the Liberation on Ike."[22]

Following the ceremony, de Gaulle invites all the city's high-ranking military and civilian representatives to a reception at the Hôtel de Ville. Diplomats have no great love of such festivities, which have a reputation for being cold,

Charles de Gaulle and his wife, Yvonne. The general became head of the provisional French government in Paris in 1944.

joyless affairs. Amusing small talk is foreign to de Gaulle's nature, so conversations with him tend to be long and drawn out. Duff Cooper and his wife, Diana, refer to the general behind closed doors as "the giraffe," a mocking reference to the fact that he is six-foot-five. Lady Diana particularly dreads encountering Yvonne de Gaulle, who is even less fond of amiable chitchat than her husband and is known as an extraordinarily strict moralist. The mere thought of having to shake hands with a divorced woman is said to be enough to give her a migraine.

"Madame de Gaulle is rather a pathetic little woman who I should think has a hard life," says Duff Cooper. "She is obviously forbidden to put on any makeup."[23] In any case, Lady Diana makes every effort to please Madame, even attempting to speak with her in French. "My French, quite deplorable as it is, flows and flounders and gets there," she will later write in her memoirs.[24] The fact that she regularly mixes up *vous* and *tu* is another matter. In any case, Lady Diana seems to be the only woman to address Charles de Gaulle with the familiar *tu*. Madame Yvonne would be mortified at such a faux pas.

Winston Churchill writes to Josef Stalin on June 15: "I suggest that we use the code word TERMINAL for the forthcoming Berlin Conference. Do you agree?"[25] Stalin has no objections.

V

In mid-June, Count Hans von Lehndorff takes up work as a surgeon at a Königsberg hospital. The thirty-five-year-old doctor endured terrible weeks of detention in a Soviet internment camp with around four thousand other men and women starting at the end of April. A few days earlier, the Red Army had conquered what little was left of the city, suffering heavy losses. Königsberg is now Soviet-occupied, and Germans like Lehndorff whom the officials of the feared People's Commissariat for Internal Affairs (NKVD) considers politically suspicious are regularly interrogated. "The point of these interrogations was not to get people to tell what they knew but to force them to make certain statements," Lehndorff would later recall. "The methods used were very primitive. People were beaten until they admitted that they were party members."[26] Many died during and after questioning, even more perished of the terrible diseases rampant in the camp. But Lehndorff is lucky. He was in fact never a member of the NSDAP, and doctors are in short supply everywhere.

The hospital where Lehndorff now has to treat his German compatriots is a horror show. Many of the patients are emaciated, little more than skeletons. "Some walk under their own power on misshapen, swollen legs and lie down in front of the door, where a lot of similar figures are already lying on makeshift stretchers or on the floor. Each time, we ask ourselves whether it makes sense to amputate the legs of these people or whether it's better to just let them die.

We usually leave it at the latter." There are enough medical instruments, medicines, and bandages available since the Germans had horded large stocks of them. "But," asks Lehndorff, "what good is all that if you can't give people anything to eat?"[27]

Hunger is the biggest problem in East Prussia. The Wehrmacht has plundered the province: entire dairies had been dismantled, water pipes destroyed, and almost all livestock and horses slaughtered. Tens of thousands of German civilians are now threatened with starvation.

"Starvation is a strange way to die," notes Hans von Lehndorff, who can usually only look on helplessly. "The people give the impression that they have already gone through death. They still walk upright, you can still talk to them, they reach for a cigarette butt—rather than a piece of bread, by the way, which they no longer know what to do with—and then they fall down all at once, like a table that holds up under maximum load until the additional weight of a fly causes it to collapse."[28]

From time to time, the doctor is also confronted with diseases he previously only knew from medical textbooks: for example, cheek gangrene—known in medical jargon as "noma"—in which a person's face is eaten away within a few days by severe bacterial infection. Where the jawbone, teeth, lips, and cheeks used to be, there is suddenly a large gaping hole, and the patient dies in severe pain.

How does Lehndorff cope with all this? His faith props him up. "To have lived a life only to die here in this place, literally in shit! A song involuntarily comes to mind: 'God has brought me this far.' Or is that a blasphemy? But who else could have done that? No, whomever He has helped up to this point, He must also help further."[29]

V

For his entire life, whenever asked about his oldest son, Hans, Commercial Councilor Falke shrugged his shoulders and not infrequently let out a deep sigh. Unfortunately, things like this happen in even the best of families, the old gentlemen is wont to say before quickly changing the subject. Councilor Falke is the owner of a leather goods factory in Cologne from which in good years several hundred earn their keep. In keeping with their social status, he and his family live in a trendy villa on Hohenzollernring boulevard, nicknamed "Millionaires' Mile." Five of the councilor's six children have made something of themselves. Hans is the black sheep, a fraud and a conman. He lies every time he opens his mouth, a fact reflected by his criminal record. He's done a total of five years in prison for false bankruptcy, fraud, embezzlement, and falsifying official documents. And as if that weren't enough, while serving a sentence in the Brandenburg-Görden prison in 1932, he exploited a mutual acquaintance to begin corresponding with twenty-five-year-old Hertha Teschke, proposing marriage, although they were complete strangers. As soon as they were wed, he promised, he would receive a significant sum of money from his parent, which he would naturally share with her. It was another utter lie. Hans in fact hoped that being a married man would help him secure an early release. Unbelievably, the young couple did wed in the prison, making Miss Teschke into Mrs. Falke. The councilor predictably didn't open the financial floodgates, and Hans wasn't freed early either. But despite having been conned, Hertha stayed with her husband when he was finally released from jail in 1935. "Our relationship wasn't very good," she will say. "That was down particularly to the fact that my husband was always trying to meet other women and would bring them to our apartment, when I wasn't home."[30]

Ten years later, on April 27, 1945, the doors of a prison open once more for Hans Falke after a six-month sentence for embezzlement. But now things are going to get better. Hans can sense the chance amid the demise of the Third Reich to reinvent himself. A short time after German capitulation, he goes to the mayor of Berlin's Schöneberg district and applies for official recognition as a victim of fascism, telling the officials that his frequent stretches in prison were the result of political persecution. In the chaos of the first days after the war, the mayor's office asks few questions and simply issues the requested documents. His wife left Berlin in the final months of the fighting for parts unknown, and Hans doesn't have anywhere to live, so he seeks out Anna Ebert, who runs a bordello in Nollendorfstrasse he has occasionally frequented. He asks if he can stay there temporarily, and she has nothing against the idea. In Ebert's establishment, he meets Anita Knoche, a twenty-eight-year-old woman who has been turning tricks there for a short while. Anita styles herself as a luxury courtesan: well-kept, polite, immaculately dressed. Somewhere she has managed to get her hands on a genuine fur coat, in which she parades through the ruins of Berlin. That makes quite an impression. In reality, Anita is a small-time criminal who has been brought up numerous times on charges of fraud. Falke is taken with her in any case, and for four weeks the two of them are inseparable. Perhaps they sleep with one another—who knows?

When darkness falls, Anita and Hans walk the bombed-out streets, climbing over piles of rubble, breaking into abandoned apartments and taking anything not nailed down. On Grossadmiral-von-Koester-Ufer, they force their way into some former offices of the Wehrmacht and steal five large typewriters. Elsewhere they pilfer cigarettes and alcohol and plunder a warehouse full of fabric. They sell what they steal on the black market. Hans trusts Anita so unreservedly that he tells her about his previous life, his stretches in prison, his marriage, and his tricking his way into being certified as a victim of fascism. He also shares his plans to start a construction company. After all, the mountains of rubble must be carted away somehow. There will be a lively market in that area, and as someone who was purportedly opposed the Third Reich and was persecuted for his convictions, he'll have an inside track on public contracts.

One late evening several weeks afterward, Hans is sitting in his newly opened office on Martin-Luther-Strasse

18 when Anita suddenly appears wearing brown trousers, a blouse, and a garish red overcoat. Neighbors and passersby notice her when she approaches the building. Hans and Anita soon get in a fight. Anita feels betrayed and demands money, which Hans refuses to hand over. One word leads to another. Anita is enraged and threatens to expose him as a fraud. She knows a lot, she threatens, and has no qualms about going to the police. She'll tell everyone that he's a common conman, not a victim of fascism. She can't do that to him, yells Hans. But Anita only laughs mockingly. She'll also tell his family the truth, she adds.

All at once, the new life upon which Hans has just embarked is in acute jeopardy. He had such lovely visions for the future as a victim of fascism and an honorable man and a business owner. Anita threatens to destroy everything. He has to silence her, he thinks, any way he can.

Hans grabs Anita, holds her mouth shut and chokes her. In the ensuing struggle, Anita falls over backward and bashes her head into a bread cutting machine attached to a table. She now lies on the floor, bleeding and gasping. Falke picks up a pair of pliers and hits Anita on the head with all his might, once, twice, thrice, until she doesn't make a sound. The following morning he'll dispose of her body in a storage space near Sachsendamm. That's his plan.

Two months later, Hans is arrested and interrogated.

"Did you think you'd be taken into custody?" he's asked.

"Yes."

"Why should you be arrested?"

"Because I'm guilty."
"With regards to what?"
"In the matter of Anita Knoche."
"So you admit you caused Anita's death"
"Yes."[31]

On June 17, the forty-four-year-old Red Army soldier Vassili Petrovich W. writes to his daughter Inotschek: "There are now more than thirty cinemas open in Berlin. The cinema employees say that there has never before been such an influx of people as there is now. Our films are shown here. And there is often applause during the screening."[32]

"This peace is a headache to all those who brought it about—except for Mr. Stalin, who takes everything he can from it," writes Alma Mahler-Werfel to her friend Friedrich Torberg on June 18. "If things stay this way, we won't be able to return for a long time."[33] She means to Vienna, Alma's hometown. When Hitler and the Germans invaded Austria in March 1938, she and her husband, writer Franz Werfel, immediately fled the country. The couple have been living in Los Angeles since early 1941, along with many other German-speaking exiles: writers Thomas and Heinrich Mann, Bertolt Brecht, Bruno Frank, Alfred Döblin, and Torberg, composers Arnold

Schönberg, Hanns Eisler, and Erich Wolfgang Korngold, directors Max Reinhardt and Fritz Kortner, philosophers Max Horkheimer and Theodor W. Adorno, to name but a few. All settled in "German California" at some point after fleeing Europe. Alma would like to return to Vienna, but for the time being the political situation in the city occupied by the Red Army still seems too uncertain. Perhaps in the fall.

Alma's first husband was composer Gustav Mahler. After his death, she married the architect Walter Gropius, before wedding her third husband Franz Werfel in 1929. She's rumored to have had many affairs—one of her lovers allegedly being a Catholic priest and Professor of Moral Theology—but nothing is known for certain. While many European refugees struggle to make ends meet in the United States, Franz and Alma live the high life. Werfel's novel *The Song of Bernadette*, published in 1942, was a bestseller in America and has greatly swelled the couple's coffers, allowing them to afford a villa in Beverly Hills. Alma is known as a generous hostess who treats life as a dizzying, enjoyable carousel ride, beguiling and charming her guests. She's at her best when her senses and mind are both intoxicated and aroused. On such occasions, Alma serves up the champagne, the most expensive wines, and the most exquisite delicacies. Even the notoriously fussy Thomas Mann writes of her "excellent hospitality."[34]

In addition to a household servant, the Werfels also employ a private secretary. Albrecht Joseph is in his early forties and comes from Frankfurt am Main. He's also a Jew, who involuntarily left Germany after Hitler gained power. After stations in Austria, Italy, England, and France, he finally succeeded in reaching the United States. Werfel and his secretary spend hours in his office, where he dictates from the black school notebooks in which he composes his novels and poems. His latest novel, *Star of the Unborn,* an idiosyncratic work of science fiction set in the year 101,943, is almost finished, which is a virtual miracle considering that Franz Werfel has suffered from a serious heart condition for the past two years.

When his work with Franz is done, Alma summons Albrecht Joseph. "Don't be such a Jew," she teases him. "Sit down and have a little glass of schnapps."[35] Alma, by nature a great fan of alcohol, is particularly fond of Bénédictine, a strong French herb liqueur distilled in a cloister in Normandy. By afternoon, the lady of the house has usually emptied her daily bottle. "Bénédictine was too sweet for me, so I had a whiskey," Albrecht will later remember. "I didn't want more than one, whereupon she would say, 'There's no drinking with you because you're a Jew.'"[36]

Albrecht is never at a loss for words, countering with the examples of notorious Jewish alcoholics like Austrian writers Joseph Roth and Egon Friedell, both of whom nearly drank themselves to death. But it's no use. Mrs. Mahler-Werfel is convinced that Jews are inferior to Gentiles, in drinking as in everything else. Although she herself fled for her life and only barely succeeded in escaping the Nazis, in American exile she acts like a crass anti-Semite. Werfel, who comes

Alma Mahler-Werfel and her third husband, Franz Werfel, help themselves to a glass of Southern Comfort from their minibar. "Don't be such a Jew. Sit down and have a little glass of schnapps."

from a Jewish family, suffers greatly from his wife's behavior. Not that long ago, in the presence of Jewish friends, Alma went so far as to say that Hitler had done "many praiseworthy things." When someone objected that "nothing could ever make the world forget the horrors which the Nazis had committed," Alma answered, "those horror stories are fabrications put out by the refugees." Albrecht later recalled: "For a moment, we all just sat there paralyzed. Then, Werfel jumped up screaming, his face a deep purple, his eyes bulging... I do not remember verbatim what he said, but it was like the thunder of one of the Old Testament prophets. He was beside himself, had completely lost control and was dangerously close to a fit of apoplexy."[37]

Such incidents lead some German emigrees like Theodor W. Adorno to avoid Alma's company, but most of them shrug off her poor behavior. In response to a left-wing friend who asked him why he still had contact to Mrs. Mahler-Werfel, Thomas Mann paused for a moment, perplexed, and then answered with a smile: "She gives me partridges to eat, and I like them."[38]

V

"It is not entirely clear to me what is being celebrated so obtrusively today," writes Thea Sternheim in her diary on June 18.[39] Since the wee hours of the morning all of Paris is in a state of excitement. No one goes to work, children have been given off from school, and patriotic music plays on the radio, interrupted time and again by the Marseillaise. Five years ago today, on June 18, 1940, from his exile in London, Charles de Gaulle called upon the French people to resist German occupation. At the time, he was a relatively unknown general who, one day after the complete defeat of the French army, spoke out eloquently against the conquerors. France had lost a battle, he warned, but not the war. "Whatever happens, the flame of French resistance must not and will not be extinguished."[40]

Five years later, de Gaulle has become the head of the provisional French government and a national hero. La Grande Nation may not have been able to free itself from the German yoke on its own—it needed the help of the Americans and the British—but it nonetheless regards itself as one of the victorious powers. To underpin this claim, de Gaulle has arranged for an impressive military parade. A good fifty thousand men march from the Arc de Triomphe along the Avenue des Champs-Élysées to the Place de la Concorde. The 2nd Armored Division, led by General Philippe Leclerc standing in a tank, leads the triumphal procession. The fact that the tank is an American M4 Sherman is only a minor distraction. There are also impressive scenes in the sky, as a low-flying French squadron of warplanes forms the Cross of Lorraine.

The self-aggrandizement rubs Allied diplomats and officers the wrong way. Many Americans and British are annoyed at having to watch "their" tanks roll by for hours and use up "their" gasoline. "But one couldn't help thinking how all these and most of the equipment was of Anglo-American origin," remarks British ambassador Duff Cooper. "Not a single English or American flag was shown. There was no evidence of an ounce of gratitude and one felt throughout that France was boasting very loud, having very little to boast about."[41]

Meanwhile, Thea Sternheim is immune to the French national exuberance. In her journal, she notes: "The way the radio intrudes upon the beautiful June morning today reminds me frighteningly of what I experienced in Germany when Hitler grabbed power. The eternal recurrences of the same. Patriotism as the seed of the most terrible plagues and epidemics."[42]

"Congratulations," says Lieutenant Colonel J. R. Foss by way of a greeting, "you've got a job you're really suited to." This is empty flattery. Foss doesn't really care who is standing in front of him. The main thing is that his counterpart is fluent in the language of America's former enemy. "Unfortunately, I can't speak a word of German, so I'm very glad you're here."[43] The man being wooed, the Austrian film director Billy Wilder, has only just landed in Frankfurt am Main from the United States as part of an American military's so-called Information Control Division. The ICD is supposed to steer intellectual life in liberated Germany, promote the development of democratic values, and dissuade Germans from National Socialism. From the airport, the group is taken by bus to Bad Homburg, about twenty kilometers away, and housed in a former school for railroad engineers. Their mission is naturally top secret, the men are told.

The newly minted soldier, about whose arrival Lieutenant Colonel Foss is so pleased, worked as a newspaper journalist and screenwriter in Berlin at the end of the 1920s. His specialty was reports on society that briskly and ironically captured the lifestyle of the Roaring Twenties in the German capital. Wilder often wrote about the highs and lows of interpersonal communication and nightlife in the city. He was hired as a ballroom dancer for three months at the posh Hotel Eden and published a multipart report about it in the *Berliner Zeitung*. No question—the guy had chutzpah. But when the Nazis came to power, he had to leave the country posthaste. Wilder is Jewish. After a brief time in Paris, he emigrated to the United States in 1934, where he made a stellar career for himself as a director in Hollywood. His film *Double Indemnity*, released in 1944, received no fewer than seven Oscar nominations, including in the categories "Best Director" and "Best Adapted Screenplay," but unfortunately he came away empty-handed.

"In Homburg, I led more the life of a bureaucrat than that of a soldier," Wilder later recalled. He worked in the ICD's "Film, Theater and Music Control Section," particularly on film. It was his job to assess artists, issue permits, impose bans, and suggest how to help German cinema get back on its feet. "When we didn't give someone a work permit, we should have thought one step further," Wilder will later say. "Why isn't he actually in prison?"[44]

At one point, the officer responsible for theater approaches Wilder. A request has been received from Oberammergau in Bavaria to hold the town's famous Passion play there again, and the colleague, who has never heard of this Bavarian religious spectacle, wants to know whether it should be allowed. Wilder does some research, asks for documents, and quickly concludes that in 1934, the last time the Passion play was staged, the ensemble, regardless of whether they were playing Romans, Jews, or Jesus's disciples, consisted largely of Nazis. Most grotesquely, this was also true of the actor in the role of Christ, Alois Lang, whose main profession was hotelier. Should a former SS man be allowed to play Jesus? After a short deliberation, Wilder replies: "You can put on your play, but on one condition. You have to use real nails."[45] The tradition of the Passion play will not be resumed until 1950, and then only over the objections of writer Arthur Miller and composer and conductor Leonard Bernstein that it be canceled because of its latent anti-Semitism.

One of the tasks of Wilder's unit is to confront the Germans with the crimes committed in their name. English and American cameramen had shot footage during the liberation of the concentration camps that showed horrific images: huge piles of corpses, survivors emaciated to skeletons. Based on it, director Hanuš Burger, who was born in Prague and also emigrated to the USA, came up with the film *The Death Mills* about the concentration camps, creating a fictional storyline especially for the film, which was staged in Hamburg at no small expense. However, those in charge deem the rough cut of the film, with its running time of eighty-six minutes, too long, and commission Wilder to shorten it. When he sees the raw material for the first time, he freezes: "There was one scene, for example, from the liberation of Bergen-Belsen that I will never forget: There was a whole field, a whole landscape of corpses. And sitting on one of the corpses was a dying man. He is the only one still moving in this valley of death, and he looks apathetically into the camera. Then he turns away, tries to get up, struggles to rise, stumbles over a corpse, falls over, and lies dead. I can still see the final look on the man's face today, the most shocking look on anyone's face I've ever seen."[46]

Wilder is touched by such images because he, too, lost family members in the Holocaust. His mother died in the Płaszów concentration camp, his stepfather in Belzec. But he thinks it's a bad idea to depict such things in a movie. When Hanuš Burger visits him in his hotel one morning to talk about the cuts, he's rebuffed. "Films have to entertain," Wilder tells him. "We're alienating them with your movie!" Burger can't believe his ears. There's really no need to take any Nazi sensitivities into consideration, he replies. But Wilder waves his hand dismissively, saying that the Germans have had enough of Nazism for generations. "And objectively speaking, as unsympathetic as they are, they may be our logical allies of tomorrow—please, I'm quoting our Uncle in Washington verbatim."[47]

It doesn't take long for Billy Wilder to shorten Burger's film. "No one wants to know any of the ancillary nonsense anyway, and they only want to experience the bare minimum of the horror stories. I don't want to see any more of that." He tells his editor: "Sam, you know how to do it yourself. Shock them—jerk some tear ducts—then shock again, and then at the end give them some reassurance that something like this can't happen again, with Eisenhower and Churchill and Truman, and Stalin for all I care, as a guarantee."[48] The final cut of the film is only twenty-two minutes long.

V

On June 22, Thea Sternheim sits in a bistro, longing for her daughter to finally show up. The door opens and a man in an American GI uniform enters the restaurant. At first Thea can't place him, but then it hits her. "He's gotten old and is no longer attractive," she thinks, then shouts across the restaurant, "Klaus, my darling!"[49] The man immediately turns around. It's Klaus Mann, who's arrived in Paris the day before on his trek through liberated Europe. Klaus sits down at the table with Thea, and the two of them strike up a conversation.

Klaus asks how France intends to deal with Philippe Pétain's supporters. As head of the Vichy regime from 1940 to 1944, the marshal collaborated with Hitler's Germany, and a trial against him is about to begin. Before Thea can answer, Klaus points to a few other bistro customers, murmuring that these people are undoubtedly "Pétainists." Thea laughs loudly, declaring in an offhand manner, "Well, in France people want to eat their fill."

"Cocteau was also a *collaboriste,* wasn't he?" counters Klaus.

"Oh," cries Thea. "You'd be better served asking whether he's any good as a poet!"[50]

Klaus refuses to let up. He tells her that a few days ago in Bonn, he met up with a mutual acquaintance, the literary scholar Ernst Robert Curtius, who had complained bitterly about the Allied air raids on German cities. "Is Curtius supposed to find the bombings pleasant?" Thea asks, shaking her head.[51]

Late that evening, alone in her apartment, Thea jots down what she's experienced that day in her private journal and thinks back to the conversation with Klaus Mann. "What a dangerous tendency among the Mannians," she writes, "to want to turn what little we have left of life into a trial in which everyone is interrogated about their political views."[52]

V

At some point, he lets go of her. Marta Hillers lies rigid on the bed, unable to form a clear thought. Before the Soviet soldier leaves the room, he laboriously digs a pack of cigarettes out of his trouser pocket and tosses it on the bedside table. Then he's gone, leaving Marta alone in the room.

Suddenly all is as quiet as a mouse. Although she knows he's left the room, she can still smell him—the stench of booze, tobacco, and horse manure. Marta sees his yellow teeth in her mind's eye and feels his disgusting breath on her skin.

Marta gets up, staggers to the bathroom, and vomits. When the urge to retch subsides, she lifts her head and looks in the small mirror above her sink. Marta is reminded of her mother proudly telling her that she was a pretty, well-formed child with her peach-colored skin. She hardly recognizes herself in the green face in her reflection, the face of a violated woman. Marta disgusts herself.

Marta Hillers is thirty-four years old and until recently has worked as a journalist in Berlin. She also has a boyfriend named Gerd, a soldier on the Eastern Front whom she hasn't heard from for nine weeks. She has recently started keeping a diary. She does this for Gerd—she writes down what has happened since then, what she has had to endure, for him.

Untold number of German women suffer the same fate as Marta Hillers. In Berlin alone, around one hundred ten thousand women and girls are raped by Soviet soldiers in the first three months after the end of the war. It is estimated that one in five got pregnant, although most of those pregnancies were terminated. "No one can imagine what mass abortions there were," one woman will recall.[53]

Terrible scenes also take place in the countryside. An eight-year-old child in Mecklenburg has to watch as the women and girls of a village hide in a nearby forest when the Red Army marches in. The soldiers threaten to burn down the entire village if the women do not return. "My uncle asked his daughter to sacrifice herself for the others."[54]

However, it is not only the soldiers of the Red Army who engage in such atrocities. Members of the American, British, and French armed forces also commit rape. Gerlinde Schnittler is on her way from Bohemia to Bad Wimpfen when she's overtaken by a US Army jeep on a country road behind Crailsheim. The two GIs in the vehicle offer the eighteen-year-old girl a lift.

Gerlinde has been on the road for days and her feet hurt, so she doesn't think twice about accepting the offer. The two soldiers speed off with her, but the jeep suddenly veers off the road. "They drove me into a dense forest and took turns raping me for hours," Gerlinde remembers. "Then they drove me to Heilbronn, which was completely destroyed, and then on to Neckarsulm, where I staggered toward the nearest house, deeply shocked, and was taken in for the night by some people who helped me."[55]

At the end of June, Marta opens her front door to find Gerd standing there. "I was feverish with joy," Marta notes.[56] But disillusionment quickly sets in. Too much has happened in the past few weeks for the two of them to resume a normal life at the drop of a hat. And what does "normal" mean anyway in times like these? When Gerd wants to sleep with her, she shies away. "I was glad when he let go of me," she writes in her diary. "For now, I'm ruined for this man."[57]

Silence and speechlessness begin to contaminate her and Gerd's relationship. She suffers from it. She wants to explain herself to her boyfriend, to make him understand what has happened to her. At some point, she hands him her handwritten diary.

"What does that mean?" asks Gerd, pointing to the abbreviation "Vltn." Marta can't help but laugh, as though she thinks the question is a joke. Is he serious? Is he just playing ignorant? "Violation," she says frankly. "What did you think?"[58] Gerd looks at her, stunned. The fact that his girlfriend was brutally raped several times by Soviet soldiers silences him. Not a word of consolation escapes his lips. Worse still, Marta gets the impression that Gerd thinks she and the other violated women voluntarily accepted their fate. "You've become as shameless as bitches in heat," he yells at one point. "All of you in this house. Don't you realize that?"[59]

A few days later, Gerd leaves the city for Pomerania with a fellow soldier. He's getting some food, he tells Marta as he leaves. She shrugs, secretly relieved. Will he return to Berlin? Marta doesn't care. "It may be hunger dampening my feelings," she writes in her journal. "I don't have time for a soul."[60] Gerd will never read these lines.

"We went to Berlin today, my wife and I," notes Karl Deutmann in his diary on June 24. "The roads have been cleared as much as possible to restore traffic on a makeshift basis." During the war, Deutmann was a security guard at a Mannesmann industrial plant, but now, like so many others, he's unemployed. He's been warned against going to Berlin because of outbreak of dysentery. Huge posters urge the population not to drink unboiled water, to ensure meat is thoroughly boiled or fried, and to bury all waste deep in the ground. "But what use is all that?" asks Deutmann. "The dead lie under the rubble, the rats are multiplying at an alarming rate, and there is a lack of medicine and alcohol. Meat was unloaded in front of a butcher's store, big pieces of half-smoked beef. But even during transport, they're covered in hundreds of fat black flies."[61]

Anyone with something to swap, trade, or sell heads for one of the many black markets across the city. The police have recently counted a good seventy places where people barter and trade, but the actual number is probably much higher. Berlin is a paradise for racketeers. The black markets on Potsdamer Platz, Kurfürstendamm, and in the area between the Brandenburg Gate, the Reichstag building and Tiergarten are particularly busy. There is nothing you can't buy there: carpets and men's wristwatches, military boots and children's shoes, potatoes and jewelry, cameras and fur coats, thermometers and women's stockings, and cigarettes, cigarettes, and more cigarettes. American Chesterfields are particularly coveted. In fact, they've become something of a second currency. Allied soldiers also frequent the black markets, with the Americans and British mainly buying watches and jewelry, while the Soviets are also interested in clothing. In addition to the agreed purchase price, they often pay with

Practically anything can be bought or sold at the black market in front of the Reichstag building in Berlin. One main form of currency is Chesterfield cigarettes.

food such as butter, sausage, bacon, sugar, and bread. Karl Deutmann recalls: "A Russian officer was sitting in a car, a knife in his hand, in front of him a container of butter. An interpreter sat opposite him, handing him watches to look over and telling the Germans how many kilos or pounds of butter or bacon or canned meat they would fetch. Food rich in fat was exchanged for items made of gold. Shoes and the like were paid for in cash."[62]

All of this is, of course, strictly forbidden and punishable by law. Recently, 429 people were arrested in raids in Mulackstrasse and Gormannstrasse in the Mitte district and taken to the police headquarters in nearby Dircksenstrasse. The Red Fortress, as the building is popularly known, suffered heavy damage in Allied air raids, but the large inner courtyard is still halfway intact and is spacious enough to accommodate large numbers of people. Those caught dealing on the black market are forced to hand over the goods they bought or exchanged and are registered as offenders, though most get off with only a fine. But police raids are spotty at best. As soon as one black market is eradicated, racketeering pops up and flourishes elsewhere.

V

"On June 24, 1945, I got up earlier than usual," notes Georgy Zhukov. "The first thing I did was to look out of the window to see if our weathermen had been correct in forecasting a cloudy sky and drizzling rain. How I wished that they should be wrong this time!"[63] Zhukov doesn't get his wish. Moscow is completely overcast, and rain pours down incessantly. This bad weather would hardly be worth mentioning if it didn't upset Stalin's plans. The largest parade in the history of the Soviet Union is due to take place this Sunday, with a good 40,000 soldiers, over 1,800 vehicles, and a military band with more than 1,300 musicians. Stalin wants to celebrate the victory over Germany with a gigantic spectacle and at the same time present himself as a military genius who has led the Red Army from victory to victory. Both of these aims are now in danger of being washed out, and the dictator is understandably not in the best of moods a few minutes before ten o'clock as he strides across Red Square to Lenin's tomb, wearing a gray military coat and a peaked cap that does little to protect his head from the rain. Water drips from the tip of his nose, but Stalin refuses to acknowledge it, not wiping his face once. When the countless spectators, who have gathered around the square despite the bad weather, catch sight of the sixty-six-year-old, a roar of cheers goes up. Stalin greets the crowd and steps onto the balcony of Lenin's Tomb, from where he will watch the action. The air show, in which warplanes were to have thundered at low altitude over Red Square, has been canceled due to poor visibility.

Shortly before the parade begins, Zhukov arrives at the Kremlin's Savior Tower on a white horse and waits for his moment. When the tower bell chimes ten, the command "Parade, halt!" rings out, and Zhukov rides through the gate onto Red Square. There he's met by Marshal Konstantin Rokossovsky, also on horseback, whom he orders to start the procession. What might Stalin be thinking? And why isn't he the one accepting the accolades? The secret nobody is allowed to know is that Stalin doesn't know how to ride. About a week ago, he made a surreptitious attempt to learn but couldn't manage the horse and got thrown. The fall left him with all kinds of bruises. As soon as he got back on his feet, he cursed and snarled "Let Zhukov inspect the parade. He's a cavalryman." When the general heard about this, he shudders at what would have otherwise been an honor. He knows how sensitive and vindictive Stalin can be. "Wouldn't it be better if you inspected the parade?" Zhukov suggests, hoping to get out of his dilemma. "After all, you are the Supreme Commander." But Stalin graciously waves him off: "I'm already too old... Do it, you're younger."[64]

At the end of the two-hour spectacle, there are suddenly hundreds of deafening drum rolls, and a unit of two hundred Red Army soldiers march toward Lenin's Tomb, holding Wehrmacht and Waffen-SS troop flags and standards, including the banner of the "Leibstandarte Adolf Hitler," the former German dictator's own personal guards. The various emblems were brought to Moscow from Berlin and Dresden especially for this occasion, although little care was taken about their provenance. The captured trophies include around twenty flags from the nineteenth century, among them two Prussian cavalry standards and a Landwehr militia

During the victory parade on Red Square in Moscow, Soviet soldiers throw captured military flags and Wehrmacht and the Waffen-SS banners to the ground.

flag from the 1860s. Nonetheless, when the soldiers turn at the tomb and throw the flags onto the muddy ground at Stalin's feet, it's an impressive bit of theater, a symbolic disposal of National Socialism, culminating with the men taking off their gloves and burning them.

On the evening of this memorable Sunday, at a banquet for around 2,500 officers, Stalin makes a toast to "the Russian people" and the "proletarians"—the ordinary folks "without whom none of us, whether marshals or commanders of fronts and armies, would be worth a damn."[65] The toast is also a warning. No one can be sure of their position in Stalin's court. Does Georgy Zhukov get the message?

V

Alfred Misselhorn is still interned as a prisoner of war in Rennes, France. On June 24, he writes in his diary: "Americans and French do the roll call together. That takes a little longer. The French are worse at counting."[66]

V

June 26, a Tuesday, begins for Thea Sternheim with a visit to the tax office. Afterward, she runs various errands and heads to one of the many small parks typical of the Parisian cityscape. Thea loves to sit outside on a bench and let her thoughts drift, or go "vagabond," as the French say. When she returns to Rue Antoine Chantin at around 5:00 p.m., the concierge Madame Druau rushes up to her. She's weeping but, Thea quickly realizes, her tears are not in sadness. Finally, Druau throws her arms around Thea's neck and exclaims "Mops" over and over again. Mopsa and a friend from Lyon have landed in Paris by plane, Thea understands. The two are expected at her place this evening.

"Again, I felt like I'd been hit over the head," Thea will remember. "I cried to myself."[67]

Mopsa and her friend will need a hearty dinner, Thea decides after getting ahold of herself. She runs to Avenue de Châtillon several times to buy the necessary ingredients in the street's stores. Around 10:00 p.m., the time has come, and the two women arrive at Thea's small apartment. For Thea, this is a moment of intoxication that fogs her feelings and thoughts. For a second, she even thinks that Mopsa has put on weight, that "the Ravensbrück pig slop" has apparently "turned to fat."[68] After dinner, Mopsa's friend collapses on a couch and immediately falls asleep. Mother and daughter retire to Thea's bed.

The two women lie side by side, and Mopsa begins to talk about her experiences in Ravensbrück—about the omnipresence of death in the concentration camp, the sadism of the guards, the torture and executions, and the many diseases rampant in the barracks. That's how they pass the night.

"How am I supposed to comprehend all these horrors, the extent of which I'm still unable to believe?" Thea records in her diary. "How are we supposed to go on living with them as a fact?"[69]

V

Hermann Kieser is also struggling with disbelief. The septuagenarian has traveled a lot in his life, worked as a missionary and managed the homes of German army and navy personnel in Turkey, but nowhere has he encountered such licentious and disgraceful behavior as recently in Künzelsau. For him, the small town in Württemberg is a cesspool of sin, although as rector of the local Protestant church district he has preached against moral decay for ten years. "Unfortunately and painfully, I repeatedly have had call to reprimand the street children for undignified begging for chocolate and girls and young women for their sometimes outrageous cozying up to the enemy soldiers," the pious gentleman writes to Superior Church Council on June 26. "The evacuees from the Rhineland in particular manifestly and completely lack the sense of decency & dignity required of a German woman in their dealings with our enemies. Repeated serious & very clear admonitions & warnings from the pulpit preaching have sadly proven mostly unsuccessful, especially since those whom they concern are usually not in church."[70]

Kieser is not alone in his disapproval. Cordial relations between US soldiers and the German population is also a thorn in the side of the military administration of the American occupying forces, albeit for different reasons. When US troops set foot on German soil in the fall of 1944 and conquered the city of Aachen, General Dwight D. Eisenhower issued a "non-fraternization order," mandating that GIs avoid contact with Germans on a friendly, familiar, or intimate basis, whether individually or in groups, whether officially or unofficially.[71]

Justifying the order, Eisenhauer cited security concerns, fears that a German underground movement might emerge and carry out acts of sabotage. Germans were also to be made aware that they had incurred the mistrust and contempt of the civilized world. Practically speaking, the ban on fraternization aims at isolating the German population from the military occupiers. For example, GIs are prohibited from having lengthy conversations—especially private conversations—with Germans and from attending sports, entertainment, and cultural events together. Soldiers aren't allowed to visit Germans in their homes, give them gifts or, conversely, accept gifts from them. They are not even allowed to shake their hands. Violations can be severely punished.

But the ban on fraternization proves to be a nonstarter. Many GIs reject the regulation as a restriction on their personal freedom and make no attempt to comply with it. By the spring of 1945, violations have reached a level that make consistent monitoring or punishment impossible. Flirtations between military personnel and German Fräuleins are growing increasingly common. "War is compounded of one tenth discomfort and nine tenths boredom, and it is the latter that over-stimulates sex in soldiers who have little else to think about," American intelligence officer Saul K. Padover laconically notes. "To a man bored and fed up with the company of other men, almost anything in skirts is a stimulant and a relief, and German women were not just skirts."[72]

General Eisenhower finally realizes that his war on fraternization cannot be won and begins an orderly retreat. Initially, he declares that the ban on contact does not extend to children, and a few weeks later—in mid-July—American soldiers are given express permission to converse with adult Germans on the streets and squares. Nine months later, the first American-German children are born. As a result, the US Army's intelligence service draws a sobering conclusion that the policy of nonfraternization, insofar as it was intended to instill a sense of collective guilt in the German population, has failed.[73]

V

At the end of June, almost 130 cinemas are in operation in Berlin. In addition to the American and British-produced newsreel *Welt im Bild*, Soviet films are often shown, including the musical *Um 6 Uhr abends nach Kriegsende* (*Six P.M.*), in which a schoolteacher and an artillery officer manage to meet at a certain time and place in the turmoil of the postwar period. Sometimes, however, cinemas also show Hollywood films discovered in Joseph Goebbels's Reich Film Archive. People long for distraction and diversion. Around one hundred thousand moviegoers flock to the cinemas every day.

V

A good seven weeks after their liberation, Margot Bendheim and Adolf Friedländer are still in the camp. "There was no reason for me to leave Theresienstadt," Margot will remember. "My friends and especially Adolf were the remaining people dearest to me. And they were all there."[74] Anyway, where were she and Adolf supposed to go? Their families were dead, and Berlin, where they had last lived, was far away and, as they heard, badly destroyed. Where could they stay in the ruins of what was once a vibrant metropolis? Perhaps their former homes no longer exist? Millions of people feel the same as Margot and Adolf. Having been abducted or expelled from their homes, they now have nowhere to turn, even as peace has finally been restored.

Margot works doing the camp laundry, Adolf in the bakery. Sometimes they leave the camp and go for a walk in the surrounding area. The Bohemian countryside with its graceful hills, lush meadows, and dark forests is very beautiful. Too good to be true, Margot thinks. At one point, they pass huge strawberry fields. "Can we pick a basket of strawberries?" Adolf asks the farmer's wife. "We'll pay too," adds Margot and hands the farmer's wife a banknote. But the woman waves her hand to dismiss the thought, saying, "Take as much as you want."[75]

A little later, when Margot and Adolf are sitting next to each other on a bench, he suddenly asks her: "Can you imagine a life with me?" Margot nods wordlessly. Is she in love?

Margot doesn't know. "I still needed time to allow myself to have feelings like that, to become a person again. For me, feelings were only associated with pain, with memories. Adolf felt the same way. Perhaps this pain brought us closer together than being in love."[76] On June 26, they were married by a rabbi according to Jewish custom. Adolf borrows a friend's trousers, as his own are worn out, and Margot sews her own wedding dress from old scraps of fabric. After the ceremony, they invite their friends for coffee and cake.

Four days later, a military policeman hands Adolf a telegram. He opens the envelope and hastily skims the lines. It's from his sister Ilse, who emigrated to New York. She must have somehow managed to locate Adolf in Theresienstadt. "Happy he [sic] is alive," it says in staccato. "I am married. What can I do for you?" The news changes everything. For Adolf, it is now clear that he has a family after all. "He was determined to emigrate," Margot will write later of the moment. "He no longer wanted to live among the people who had murdered his mother."[77]

In San Francisco a political conference of historical world significance comes to an end. One observer describes it as "the most important gathering since the Last Supper."[78] That may be a bit of an exaggeration, but the 850 delegates from fifty nations, who negotiated in the opera house of the West Coast metropolis since April 25, had indeed set their sights high.

The League of Nations, founded in 1920, had been unable to prevent the Second World War, and they now wanted to create a new international organization, the United Nations, which would ensure the peaceful coexistence of mankind in the long term. The UN Charter was unanimously adopted on the evening of June 25 and signed in a solemn ceremony the following day. The document with its 111 articles is a bit like a constitution, and it requires all signatories to respect each other as sovereign states and refrain from the threat or first use of military force. The UN has tasked itself with promoting international cooperation to solve humanitarian, economic, social, and cultural problems. The Charter also enshrines the protection of human rights and fundamental freedoms regardless of race, gender, language, and religion.

One political observer in San Francisco was the journalist William L. Shirer, who lived in Berlin in Nazi Germany between 1934 and 1940 as an American correspondent and was able to closely observe the everyday terror of the "Third Reich." Shirer hopes the newly founded United Nations will be nothing less than an institution that can maintain world peace: "The time is late. Another war, with its giant rockets and flying bombs—will no doubt finish the human race. This is probably our last chance to save ourselves!"[79]

One day after the Charter of the United Nations is solemnly signed in San Francisco, Alfred Misselhorn notes in his diary: "The tricolor flies from the flagpole. First roll call with Frenchmen only. There are problems. One of the German camp leaders has to step in to help. He walks through the ranks and helps to arrive at the right number. It takes a little longer the first time. The food is still good with leftovers from the American stocks. Entertaining evening organized by performers from the camp. It was quite good."[80]

Berliners are getting married again. While only 873 couples tied the knot in April 1945, including Adolf and Eva Hitler, née Braun, that number rises to 2,710 by June.

The first Berlin restaurants reopen only weeks after the end of the Second World War. Here, people enjoy themselves in a street café in front of the former Hotel am Zoo.

WINNERS AND LOSERS

Gustav Senftleben has endured a great deal of suffering in his almost twenty-five years of life. Even as a small child, his father regularly beats him up. When Senftleben Senior is drunk, which is almost every day, he's particularly vicious, frequently flying into a violent rage and striking his defenseless son with anything he can get his hands on. If Gustav's mother intervenes, he hits her too. In a rare moment of sobriety, the old man realizes that he'll beat his son to death one day and agrees to give him up for foster care. Gustav is six years old.

The Thieles, with whom Gustav goes to live, are simple farmers in a village of three hundred inhabitants east of Frankfurt an der Oder. They don't have much time to look after the needs of their foster son, but they treat him decently and teach him to live a God-fearing life. Gustav helps his aunt and uncle, as he calls them, on the farm and only attends a single year of school. At the age of fourteen, Gustav decides to leave. The Thieles have been good to him, he tells his biological mother, with whom he has occasional contact, but now he wants to stand on his own two feet. "You have to know your own mind," his mother replied tersely. "The main thing is that you get by."[1]

That's easier said than done. The two hundred marks Gustav receives for his confirmation are quickly used up. He has to earn money, but what use is someone like him who can barely write his own name? Gustav is a strong boy, however. He's good at pitching in and doesn't shy away from work. So he ends up as an agricultural laborer, moving from one farm to the next, staying in one job for six months and the next for just a few weeks. Although Gustav knows from his father what alcohol can do to a person, he too occasionally drinks more than is good for him. Under the influence of booze, he quickly becomes irritable and hot-tempered, and in no time at all, fists can fly.

In February 1941, at the age of twenty, Gustav gets drafted into military service. After a short period of training, he is sent to the eastern front, where he promptly gets shot, forcing doctors to amputate two fingers on his left hand. When Gustav has halfway recovered, he's fitted with an orthopaedic glove and sent to Nazi-occupied Poland. There he witnesses the Jewish population being deported and murdered. He decides to desert the army at the next opportunity.

He flees aimlessly through Silesia, staying with farmers or sleeping outdoors. Finally, he makes it to Berlin and seeks out his favorite sister, Frieda, putting her in great danger. But he can't stay with her. Should he be discovered, she would also face legal persecution. Gustav goes into hiding in the Reich capital, lying low in subway shafts and bombed-out houses. He's lucky at first and meets other deserters who give him food. Then, in mid-December 1944, he's picked up, arrested, and transferred to Torgau, where the Reich court martial has been relocated. The military judges make short work of his case, sentencing Gustav Senftleben to death in the spring of 1945. But the war ends before the sentence can be carried out.

Gustav can't believe that he, who has been dealt such a bad hand by fate since his earliest childhood, has suddenly been so lucky. He has survived the damn war! For him, the fall of the Third Reich means liberation from his previous existence. He wants to start all over again, get a proper job and maybe even start a family at some point.

On July 5, Gustav returns to Berlin, where he once again seeks out his sister, hoping to find shelter for the time being, but when he knocks on the door of the left-hand ground-floor apartment in the side wing of the second courtyard of Weberstrasse 49, it's not Frieda who answers, but a man in his seventies. The stranger introduces himself as her lodger Paul Oede. Frieda left Berlin weeks ago, he says, and unfortunately, he doesn't know where she is. Gustav asks if he can stay anyway. Paul Oede nods and invites him in. There is a second man in the kitchen, who calls himself Erich Zernikow and lives in the basement of the same house. They want to raise a glass, says one of the men and points to the two bottles of schnapps on the kitchen table. Gustav should join them for a drink.

Why doesn't he just turn down the offer? He knows alcohol isn't good for him. He could excuse himself by referring to the events of the past few weeks, especially as he wants to start a new life. Instead, he nods and sits down at the table with the men. The first sip burns his throat. Potato schnapps, Gustav thinks, but by the second glass he gets used to it. Before he knows it, everything is spinning.

The more booze is consumed, the less Erich Zernikow can keep his fingers to himself. He grabs Gustav and tries to stroke him. "Hey, what are you playing at?" Gustav barks at him. "Are you flirting with me?"[2] When they've drained two bottles of schnapps, Paul Oede falls into his bed, comatose. The other two haven't had enough yet and go to Zernikow's basement apartment, but there's no alcohol there, so they set off to try their luck elsewhere. He knows a pub nearby, Zernikow slurs, but when they get there, they discover that the place has been bombed out. They move on through the neighboring streets.

What happens next is shrouded in the thick fog of intoxication. Gustav Senftleben and Erich Zernikow get into a fight on the corner of Gollnow and Landsberger Strasse. Afterward Gustav can't remember what triggered the argument. In any case, he picks up a brick and throws it at his opponent's head. Zernikow falls to the ground, Gustav bends over him and hits him several times with the brick. As Zernikow struggles to defend himself, Gustav pulls out a knife. The forensic autopsy report will later record nine stabs to the chest and one to the face.

A few days later, Gustav Senftleben is arrested. "If I had found my sister Frieda in her apartment, it would probably never have come to this crime," he tells the police.[3] Gustav's new life has lasted just a few weeks.

V

On the Thursday of Erich Zernikow's death in Berlin, general elections are held in the United Kingdom for the first time since 1935. Voting was suspended during the Second World War, with the country being governed by a wartime coalition since May 1940. The prime minister was Conservative MP Winston Churchill, and Clement Attlee, the leader of the socialist Labour Party, acted as his deputy. Churchill would like to have postponed the elections until after Japan's surrender, but his deputy refused to go along. The war was over in Europe, the Labour Party insists, and Churchill—whatever his many merits—is a man of yesterday. It's time now to shape the future. It's a clever argument, one which appeals to the British people's desire to leave behind the war and everything associated with it.

Attlee's campaign platform features various promises—from the nationalization of the economy to the introduction of a national health service—popular with voters. As expected, Churchill disagrees with them. But after the victory over Hitler's Germany what does the now seventy-year-old prime minister stand for exactly? Not even he himself knows what he wants to tell voters. "I am worried about this damned election," Churchill confesses to his personal physician Lord Moran. "I have no message for them now."[4] During the war, he always knew what was important, but now he cannot seem to deflect Labour's popular rhetoric. Instead, the prime minister decides to go on the attack. "No socialist government, conducting the entire life and industry of the country, could afford to allow free, sharp, or violently worded expressions of public discontent," he asserted in a radio address. "They would have to fall back on some form of *Gestapo*, no doubt very humanely directed in the first instance."[5]

That made more than a few listeners in front of the radio at the time exchange quizzical glances. Did Churchill really say that? Is he seriously suggesting that Labour wants to set up a new Gestapo—especially now with more and more reports about the Nazi reign of terror coming to light? Confidants of the prime minister are embarrassed by his words. Churchill's daughter Mary calls them "cheap," while keen observers such as Lord Moran see them as a sign of something fundamental.[6] For Churchill's personal physician, it is obvious that the prime minister no longer reaches people: "He has a feeling that he is back in the thirties, alone in the world, speaking a foreign tongue."[7]

After the election Churchill gets some breathing room—for a little while at least. With the ballots of soldiers stationed abroad remaining to be collected and brought to Britain, the result of the vote isn't announced until three weeks later, on July 26, 1945. Accompanied by his wife, Clementine, and Mary, Churchill travels to the small French town of Hendaye on the Spanish border to gather his strength for the forthcoming conference with Truman and Stalin. He gets a good night's sleep, gets up around midday and first takes a dip in the sea, as his private secretary recalls: "The Prime Minister floated, like a benevolent hippo, in the middle of a large circle of protective French policemen who had duly donned bathing suits for the purpose."[8] He then sits down in front of his easel in the bay of Saint Jean-de-Luz and paints. "I did not need to prepare myself for the Conference, for I carried so much of it in my head," he writes succinctly in his memoirs, "and was happy to cast it off, if only for a few fleeting days."[9]

V

The identity of the dead man found in the abandoned railway guard's house in Karlshorst in June has yet to be established. Nobody has reported him missing, and the killer is still unknown. Is the victim the SS man shown in the blurry photo? Was he perhaps sent to meet his Maker by a member of the Red Army? The Cyrillic note provides no further clues. The case is shelved.[10]

V

On Wednesday, July 11, Alfred Misselhorn notes in his diary: "Two men from our barracks have found a night job in the kitchen of an American barracks. Can eat themselves silly. Drive the whole barracks crazy with their stories. The leftovers could feed a company. They'd get punished if they take anything with them. They only give away their rations here in the camp."[11]

V

Adolf Friedländer turns thirty-five years old on July 15. He and his wife, Margot, have left Theresienstadt and are now somewhere in Bavaria in a camp for "displaced persons" (DPs), which is what the Allies call people who were deported and imprisoned by the Nazis during the war and haven't been able to return to their countries of origin. The number of DPs in the territory of the former Third Reich alone is estimated at around eleven million. Most of them are former slave laborers, concentration camp prisoners such as the Friedländers, and prisoners of war.

The United Nations Relief and Rehabilitation Administration (UNRRA), the emergency relief and reconstruction organization founded in 1943 by the nations that had banded together against Hitler, looks after these people, organizing food, clothing, and accommodation. While the local population often receives little more than 1,200 calories a day, the DPs are usually entitled to at least 2,000 calories.

The inhabitants of the camp Mr. and Mrs. Friedländer are in now call it "Camp Windsor." Margot is puzzled by the name, but no one has any explanation for it. Life there is bleak, with women and men housed separately in primitive barracks. After a few days, Adolf and a few other inmates complain to the camp management, who meekly admit that the facility is hopelessly overcrowded. "They come from everywhere," complains one of the UNRRA employees. "From the concentration camps, from the streets, even from the forests. There are just too many of them."[12]

What's more, Jewish DPs, particularly in Bavaria, are treated harshly. The American military governor George S. Patton makes no secret of his contempt for Jews. Others may think, he writes in his diary, that the DP is a human being, "which he is not, and this applies particularly to the Jews, who are lower than animals. I remember once at Troina in Sicily, General Gay said that it was not a question of the people living with the dirty animals, but of the animals living with the dirty people. At that time, he had never seen a displaced Jew."[13] Large number of DPs, who until recently were still prisoners in Nazi concentration camps, find themselves fenced in again by barbed wire and watched over by armed guards after their liberation.

Adolf and Margot are relieved when they soon get transferred to a DP camp in Deggendorf on the Danube. The red brick building in the town park was once the district mental hospital, then a barracks, and now it is the accommodation for around one thousand Jewish survivors of Nazi terror. The facilities are much better than in "Camp Windsor." There's a school for the children, a prayer room and a ritual bath, as well as a general store and a theater. In summer, the residents put on the popular play *Im weissen Rössl* ("The White Horse Inn") there. Forty-one-year-old Eugen Deutsch from Brno used to work as an emcee in Vienna, so he has stage experience and takes on the role of director. Everyone contributes what they can to the production. Costumes are sewn and stage sets constructed, props procured, and spotlights installed. In the end, there are more than thirty people on stage. *Im weissen Rössl* was therapy, for both us and the audience," Margot later comments.[14]

Most of the camp residents intend to leave Germany as soon as possible. The Friedländers want to go to the United States, while Eugen Deutsch wants to join his brother-in-law in Australia. They've been told, however, that it could take months to obtain the necessary papers. And so, little by little, something like normality returns to the lives of Margot and Adolf Friedländer. The camp even has a weekly newspaper in Yiddish and its own internal currency, the "Deggendorf Dollar." But what does normality mean in the summer of 1945?

Margot often thinks about her mother, Auguste. "My mother only left me one piece of wisdom: 'Try to make a life for yourself.' Her wish had come true. She guided me, and she held a protective hand over me. Now I began to take my new life into my own hands."[15]

V

When Heinz Zellermayer gazes over Steinplatz in Berlin, it almost brings tears to his eyes. Wherever he looks, there is nothing but bombed out buildings. The area around the rectangular park in the Charlottenburg district, which was laid out in 1885, was once one of the finest addresses in the city center. The district was known for a certain sophistication and exoticism, with many Russians who fled the revolution in their homeland in the 1920s having settled in the magnificent apartment buildings between Kurfürstendamm boulevard in the south and Bismarckstrasse to the north. Charlottenburg's nickname became "Charlottengrad," and Steinplatz was its center. The streets teemed with deposed grand dukes, elegant countesses, and all sorts of other aristocrats, some of whom likely first acquired their noble-sounding titles in exile.

The building at Steinplatz 4 was a particularly fine example of Wilhelminian architecture. Built in 1907 by the Art Nouveau architect August Endell, it housed the Hotel am Steinplatz until the building was requisitioned by the navy in 1943 as a command center for the German submarine fleet. Less than a year later, after the military had moved back out, two bombs caused considerable damage. Since then, the building has lain dormant, and the wind and weather are taking their toll. Soon, if nothing is done, it will have to be demolished. Heinz wants to prevent this at all costs. Steinplatz 4 is his childhood home.

Almost thirty years old, Heinz is an imposing figure: tall, broad-shouldered, and so unshakably self-confident it's almost dizzying. After graduating from high school, he attended the renowned hotel management school in Lausanne and then apprenticed with the legendary Otto Horcher. Horcher's eponymous restaurant on Berlin's Lutherstrasse was considered by many gourmets to be the best restaurant in Europe. The poulard, pheasant, and saddle of venison, prepared in front of diners, were miniature works of art. But as Germany's fortunes in the war worsened in 1943, Horcher had to close his gourmet temple. The situation was different in German-occupied Paris, where the enterprising restaurateur, who had excellent contacts with the National Socialist elite, had already taken over the restaurant Maxim's, the wine shop Sandeman, and the nightclub Bagatelle. Maître Otto needed a deputy there and eventually sent Heinz to the Seine. In the middle of the Second World War, the young man became the manager of what was probably the most famous restaurant in France. Horcher's Parisian establishments were mainly frequented by high-ranking members of the Wehrmacht and more or less corrupt businessmen. When gun-toting racketeers approached Heinz and demanded protection money, he successfully dispatched them, making sure that his refusal to back down did not go unnoticed. The criminals were never seen again, and the French nicknamed Heinz "Le Grand Manitou."[16]

One thing Heinz learned from Otto Horcher is that no matter how tough the times, there are always people who have money, lots of it, and appreciate good food. So what could be more obvious, he thinks to himself in the summer of 1945, than to open a luxury restaurant in the style of the old Horcher in war-torn Berlin. The first thing he needs is staff. Through an acquaintance, he gets to know Franz, who had served for many years as the butler to Alexander von Dörnberg, the former head of protocol at the Foreign Office. Franz not only has the perfect manners to be expected of a top-class restaurant manager; he's also not afraid of rolling up his sleeves and getting his hands dirty. Together, Heinz Zellermayer and his new colleague clear out the building on Steinplatz, shovel rubble, paint walls, and repair the worst damage to the façade and roof. They restore the kitchen and redo the hotel's former library on the second floor with furniture they found somewhere as the new dining room. A handful of former Horcher waiters and cooks completes the team.

A July 15 city council ordinance allows restaurants to operate—initially only at lunchtime, but it's a start. The declaration states: "Restaurants are currently not bound by regulations regarding the type of food served and the composition of the dishes. [. . .] The prices must be in line with the usual prices in Berlin before hostilities broke out."[17] This is the moment Heinz has been waiting for. One day later, Restaurant Zellermayer opens its doors.

"The first day, I organized 1 kg of meat and a tin of green beans," Heinz will later remember.[18] Hardly opulent, but necessity is the mother of invention. Heinz grows mushrooms in the cellar and tomatoes in the makeshift rooftop garden. To be able to offer his guests tea, he climbs linden trees and collects their blossoms. Heinz buys a goat for five thousand marks, which he names Beate and which provides one and a half liters of creamy milk every day, which the cook uses to create rich sauces. Pens for rabbits and chickens are set up in the courtyard. But the most important sources of various kinds of food and drink are the black market and displaced persons, who enjoy preferential treatment by the Allies. "They came by my brother's building every morning and sold him tinned fruit and vegetables as well as fresh meat," Heinz's sister, Ilse, will recall.[19] Such people also trade in coffee, spirits, diamonds, and even gasoline. Such transactions are officially prohibited, of course, and Heinz knows he'll be checked on, but he can usually spot the inspectors a mile away. On one occasion, his keen sense for trouble fails him. A patron takes his seat, and the head waiter praises the caviar and châteaubriand on that day's menu. When the inspector identifies himself and threatens repercussions, the head waiter leans over and whispers in his ear with a smile: "If you rat us out here, I'll kill you." Heinz—"Le Grand Manitou"—adds with a serious expression: "If he sees red, I can't vouch for what he'll do."[20] The inspector was never seen in the restaurant again.

It doesn't take long for the establishment's few tables to be permanently booked out. One of the first regular customers is Walter Forstreuter, chairman of the Gerling insurance group. The General Director, as the waiters address him, always wants the table by the fireplace and the special, slightly smaller than normal silver cutlery. His wishes are of course granted. "Even if we weren't able to completely match Horcher's cuisine," Heinz can still remember decades later, "what we offered was still first-class—and that goes for the prices too."[21]

V

From Alfred Misselhorn's diary, Sunday, July 15, 1945: "In the last few days, we've had to turn out to several roll calls stripped to the waist. The French are also looking for SS men—it's said, for the Foreign Legion. If sufficient pressure is applied to the prisoners, they can quickly obtain good soldiers. What anyone has done in the past no longer matters. A holding camp for Foreign Legion volunteers has been set up right next to our own. It's no wonder given our poor rations, that many sign up. Perhaps the French are saving themselves a major recruitment campaign this way. You can see that these inmates aren't going hungry."[22]

V

Early in the afternoon on July 15, Griebnitzsee lake lies calm. There is virtually no wind, and the water is as smooth as a mirror reflecting the glistening sunlight. Berlin's main city forest begins on the northern shore of this approximately three-kilometer-long lake, while the Neu-Babelsberg villa colony, which is part of the city Potsdam, adorns the southern shore. It is here in the coming weeks in this elegant area with its grand estates, many of which look like small castles, that the "Big Three"—Harry S. Truman, Winston Churchill, and Josef Stalin—will dictate the course of world history.

If Stalin had gotten his way, the conference, codenamed "Terminal," would have taken place in Berlin, but that idea was quickly abandoned as the ruins of the former capital of the Third Reich proved unsuitable for such an event. Although Potsdam was attacked by 488 British bombers in mid-April, the Babelsberg villas escaped without major damage. The nearby Cecilienhof Palace is also a sufficiently prestigious site. Last but not least, many among the Allies regard the Prussian royal seat of Potsdam as the cradle of German militarism—where, if not there, could it be more symbolically laid to rest?

Meanwhile, the Gatow airfield, located around ten kilometers north of Griebnitzsee, is a hive of activity. Next to the runway, the 2nd US Armored Division, aptly nicknamed "Hell on Wheels," has arrived. Jeeps and limousines drive up, and you can make out the Secretary of War Henry L. Stimson, his colleague John Jay McCloy, Lieutenant General Lucius D. Clay, US ambassador in Moscow William Averell Harriman, the commander of the American sector in Berlin, Floyd Lavinius Parks, Soviet ambassador in Washington Andrei Gromyko, and other diplomats and military leaders.

Change of the guard: A Soviet military policewoman directs traffic in front of Berlin's Brandenburg Gate.

It is scorching hot. Some of those present pull their hats low over their faces so that the brims cast shadows. Suddenly, at around 3:50 p.m., the sound of engines can be heard, quiet at first, getting closer and louder. A few minutes later, a Douglas VC-54C aircraft touches down on the tarmac. When the "Sacred Cow," as the plane is nicknamed, comes to a standstill, the door opens, and a smiling Harry S. Truman walks down, amiably greeting those in attendance. He's wearing a gray double-breasted suit, a matching hat, and two-tone shoes. The US President is welcomed by Minister Stimson and the other dignitaries and then immediately walks down the line of honor before heading to Griebnitzsee at around 4:30.

Haus Erlenkamp has hosted many illustrious guests over the past decades, but never an American president. The villa, built in 1890–91 in the style of an English country house, once belonged to the Müller-Grote publishing family, who had made their money from paperback editions of German classics. The property would survive the war intact, but the Müller-Grotes were driven out by the Red Army's advance into Potsdam. When Truman gets his initial look at "The Little White House," as the accommodation is henceforth known, his first impulse is to turn on his heel. "They've erected a couple of tombstone chimnies on each side of the porch facing the lake so they would cover up the beautiful chateau roof and tower," he writes mockingly in his diary. "Make the place look like hell, but purely German—just like the Kansas City Union Station." Truman was equally

During the Potsdam Conference, US President Harry S. Truman and his aides reside in Haus Erlenkamp. The villa is located on an enchanting spot on Griebnitzsee lake, but Truman is less than enthusiastic about the furnishings: "It is comfortable enough all round, but what a nightmare it would give an interior decorator."

unimpressed with the interior. Soviet soldiers had looted the villa, so he has to make do with furniture cobbled together in a hurry from wherever. "Nothing matches," he grumbles. "We have a two-ton German sideboard in the drawing room and French or Chippendale table and chairs—maybe a mixture of both. There is a birdseye maple wardrobe and an oak chest matching the two-ton sideboard in my bedroom. It is comfortable enough all round, but what a nightmare it would give an interior decorator."[23]

Churchill arrives in Gatow at around 6:00 p.m. from Bordeaux, accompanied by his daughter, Mary. He's met by Field Marshal Bernard Montgomery. The prime minister wears the army uniform of an honorary colonel of the 4th/5th Battalion of the Royal Sussex Regiment. As he descends the gangway with a cigar in his mouth, he spreads his fingers to form the "V" for victory sign. The two men stride through the guard of honor that has lined up on the shaggy lawn. At Griebnitzsee, Churchill moves into the neoclassical Villa Urbig, built by famed architect Mies van der Rohe between 1915 and 1917 for the banker Franz Urbig. Like Truman's and Stalin's villas, this stately abode is located directly on the banks of Griebnitzsee and seems also to have been the target of looters. In any case, if Churchill's personal physician is to be believed, the furnishings are sparse. On his tour of the house, the prime minister passes through bare rooms with large chandeliers and opens fingerprint-stained glass doors until he reaches the terrace. From there, he has a beautiful view of the idyllic lake. Churchill sinks into a garden chair between two pots of blue, pink, and white hydrangeas, exhausted. He still feels the arduous journey from the south of France in his bones. "Get me a whisky," he tells his aide-de-camp.[24]

As if having an inkling that the British election might not go well for him, Churchill has invited his rival, Clement Attlee, to join the British delegation. The sixty-two-year-old Labour leader is not particularly popular among British diplomats, as the influential foreign policy expert Alexander Cadogan writes to his wife: "Then, several houses further on, is a drab and dreary little building destined to house Attlee! Very suitable, it's just like Attlee himself!"[25]

Stalin, on the other hand, resides in Villa Herpich, which was built in 1910 and 1911 by Alfred Grenander for the owner of the furrier C. A. Herpich & Sons. It has two floors plus an attic and fifteen rooms covering four hundred square meters. A total of sixty-two villas have been made available to the Soviet delegation, and the dictator was briefed in detail in advance about the conditions he would find in Potsdam. "Supplies of game, poultry, gastronomic and overseas goods as well as other products and drinks have been provided," assured secret service chief Lavrentiy Beria. "Additional food production sites have been set up seven kilometers from Potsdam, with animal and poultry farms, vegetable fields, and two bakeries in operation. All the staff are from Moscow. Two special airports are ready. Seven regiments of NKVD troops, and one-and-a-half operational team members are available for security."[26]

But Comrade Stalin rejects Beria's suggestion that he travel to Germany by plane. The sixty-six-year-old dictator mistrusts air travel and is also paranoid about attacks, constantly fearing for his life. Stalin therefore decides to travel the almost two thousand kilometers from Moscow to Potsdam in a special armored train. Beria posts six to fifteen security men per kilometer of the route, 18,500 guards in total. Since Potsdam lies within the Soviet occupation zone, Beria and his men are responsible for the logistics and security of all the conference participants there. The entire route from Griebnitzsee to Cecilienhof Palace is lined with soldiers posted every six meters, and another row of guards stands ready about fifty meters behind this line of defense. The men are armed to the teeth. It's almost impossible to get into the security zone. Soviet traffic policewomen with flags stand at every intersection and on all of Potsdam's larger squares. The young women wear sleek army uniforms and move so gracefully they could pass for ballerinas. Of course, they don't have much to do, as the streets are virtually deserted during the conference.

But where is the Soviet dictator? Stalin, who has had himself named "Generalissimus," or General of Generals, after the Moscow victory parade, keeps everyone waiting on the morning of July 16. By 11:00 a.m., it becomes clear that the conference cannot begin as planned that afternoon, and Churchill pays Truman a visit in his villa to discuss the next steps. Churchill has a reputation as a late riser, as Truman uncomprehendingly notes: "His daughter told General

Vaughan he hadn't been up so early in ten years!"[27] Truman has already been awake for four-and-a-half hours.

Churchill and Truman have only met once before, fleetingly in Washington, and have never spoken personally. Now they come face-to-face, two leaders whose backgrounds could not be more different. Churchill was born into a venerable British aristocratic family, while Truman was the son of humble farmers. In 1920 Truman opened a haberdashery in Kansas City that went bankrupt a short time later, whereas by that point Churchill had already been working as a government minister for years. While many contemporaries see Churchill as a war hero and a living legend, Truman seems like a president who only came into office accidentally due to the sudden death of his predecessor. Yet despite their great differences, the two hit it off straightaway, with the prime minister particularly appreciating the new president's laconic but energetic, pragmatic manner. And vice versa? "He is a most charming and a very clever person," Truman writes in in his diary. "He gave me a lot of hooey about how great my country is and how he loved Roosevelt and how he intended to love me etc. etc."[28]

When Churchill leaves the "Little White House," Truman turns to his mail. As he sits at his desk, looking out over Griebnitzsee, a good nine thousand kilometers away near the small American town of Alamogordo in the state of New Mexico, something that will alter world history is about to take place. There, in the middle of the desert, a metal sphere is mounted on a thirty-meter-high steel tower. The sphere is covered in cables and wires, looking like something that could have been assembled in Dr. Frankenstein's laboratory. The monster, in this case, is called "The Gadget," but it's anything but as run-of-the-mill as its code name tries to suggest. This is a bomb with a plutonium core, created by forty-one-year-old Julius Robert Oppenheimer, who studied chemistry and physics at Harvard and Göttingen and has been the scientific director of the American nuclear research project—codenamed the Manhattan Project—since 1942. Scores of scientists, engineers, and military personnel wait in bunkers for the early morning test detonation. In a few minutes, the Gadget, the world's first atomic bomb, will be detonated. Oppenheimer is nervous. He hasn't slept properly in days, drinking gallons of black coffee and smoking one cigarette after another. The twenty-minute countdown begins, read out by Samuel K. Allison, a physicist from Oppenheimer's team. During the final few minutes, most of the observers lie on the ground with their feet pointed toward the bomb and simply wait. "Lord, these affairs are hard on the heart," Oppenheimer says quietly to himself as the countdown nears its last seconds.[29] He stares blankly into space, his nerves stretched to breaking point. "Three, two, one..." at 5:29 and 21 seconds a.m. local time, Allison shouts "Now!" into the microphone.

"The whole country was lighted by a searing light with the intensity many times that of the midday sun," says

General Thomas F. Farrell, the deputy commander of the Manhattan Project, describing the explosion. "It was golden, purple, violet, gray and blue. It lighted every peak, crevasse and ridge of the nearby mountain range with a clarity and beauty that cannot be described but must be seen to be imagined."[30]

The explosion has the force of twenty-one kilotons of conventional TNT and leaves behind a crater three meters deep and 330 meters wide. The shock wave can be felt 160 kilometers away, and a cloud resembling a gigantic mushroom rises twelve kilometers into the air. At the center of the detonation, the temperature rises to several million degrees, vaporizing the steel tower in an instant and turning the desert sand into greenish glass. "We knew the world would never be the same again," Oppenheimer recalls of that moment. "A few people laughed, a few people cried. Most were silent." He himself recalled a line from the *Bhagavad Gita,* one of the central Hindu scriptures: "Now I have become death, the destroyer of worlds."[31] Oppenheimer's colleague Kenneth Bainbridge puts things more bluntly: "Now we are all sons of bitches."[32]

Truman has no idea of the outcome of the test when he and Churchill each decide, independently of one another, to take advantage of their unexpected free time while waiting for Stalin's arrival by visiting Berlin. At 3:30 p.m., Truman sets off for the capital of the former Third Reich in an open car, followed by his two aides and various intelligence officers and military policemen. The convoy stops at Hitler's former New Reich Chancellery on Vossstrasse, among other places. One of those present asks if the president wants to get out and see the building, but Truman waves him off. "Never did I see a more sorrowful sight," he writes in his diary, "nor witness retribution to the nth degree."[33] But a sight Truman found even more terrible was the many people wandering aimlessly through the fetid ruins. "We saw old men, old women, young women, children from tots to teens, carrying packs, pushing carts, pulling carts, evidently ejected by the conquerors, and carrying what they could of their belongings to nowhere in particular."[34]

Churchill arrives at what's left of the Reich Chancellery about an hour later. Unlike Truman, the prime minister gets out of his jeep and walks a few meters around the building, much to the horror of his bodyguards. "Some of the crowd looked away, others glanced at him with expressionless faces, one old man shook his fist, a few smiled," remarks Lord Moran.[35] While the external damage is slight, the building's interior is a picture of devastation. The precious palisander and rosewood paneling in Hitler's four-hundred-square-meter study has been torn out and presumably burned as firewood. Shards of broken glass carpet the floor, Hitler's desk, which he hardly ever used, lies overturned, and medals and insignia are scattered among papers and burnt books. The Red Army soldier who guides

Churchill and his entourage through the ruins also shows them the entrance to the Führer's underground bunker. Churchill follows him down a flight of stairs with a cigar in his mouth, but when the soldier reveals how far there is still to go down, the prime minister turns around and returns to the courtyard with heavy steps. There he sits down on a wobbly chair in the rubble. Churchill is out of breath and wipes the sweat from his brow. "Hitler must have come out here to get some air," he says, "and heard the guns getting nearer and nearer."[36] When Lord Moran askes his prime minister later that evening for his impressions of Berlin, Churchill replied impishly: "There was a reasonable amount of destruction."[37]

V

Henry L. Stimson is a man of the past. That might sound like an insult, but he himself would probably not object to that description. Born in New York in 1867, Stimson is virtuous, deeply religious, and equipped with strong moral convictions—for many he's the personification of the nineteenth century. He firmly believes in the good in people and is fond of saying: "The only way to get a man to trust you is to trust him, and show your trust."[38] As Minister of War, Stimson's policies are level-headed and strategically astute. For example, when his cabinet colleague Treasury Secretary Henry Morgenthau presented a draft in the summer of 1944 calling for Germany, once defeated, to be transformed into a defenseless agrarian state, Stimson would hear nothing of the sort. An impoverished country whose people would be condemned to live permanently at subsistence level, he feared, would be almost impossible to control. In the end, President Roosevelt rejected Morgenthau's idea in less time than the treasury secretary had taken to write it down. Toward the end of the war, Stimson also expressed regret at what he saw as the senseless destruction of cities such as Hamburg and Dresden.

It is thus an irony of history that at 7:30 p.m., the seventy-seven-year-old secretary of war, of all people, is the one to hand a letter classified "top secret" to the US president. Back in the "Little White House," Truman immediately opens and scans the dispatch. "Operated on this morning," Truman reads. "Diagnosis not yet complete but results seem satisfactory and already exceed expectations."[39]

"On July 17, the conference of the 'Big Three,' Truman, Churchill, and Stalin, begins," Annemarie von Duhn notes in her diary. Annemarie and her husband, Johann, live in Potsdam's Babelsberg district not far from Cecilienhof Palace. She's a musician, he a physicist. Josef Stalin has finally arrived in the city. "All the roads are closed, all the traffic floods past our house."[40] Shortly after his arrival late this Tuesday morning, Stalin visits Truman in his villa. He regrets the delay, Stalin explains, but important negotiations with the Chinese kept him in Moscow, and when he was about to board his plane, his doctors forbade him to fly, so he had to take the train. This is an outright lie. Stalin no doubt deliberately kept the conference participants waiting to demonstrate his importance and show who was in charge in Potsdam. After exchanging the usual greetings, Stalin makes to leave, but Truman asks him to stay for lunch. Unfortunately, Stalin demurs, he's unable to do that. "You could if you wanted to," Truman insists rather undiplomatically.[41] This seems to impress Stalin, who changes his mind. "I can deal with Stalin," Truman later confides in his diary. "He is honest—but smart as hell."[42]

A few hours later, Stalin will provide the first evidence of his cunning. At around 5:00 p.m., the conference participants enter the former residential hall of Cecilienhof Palace and take their seats at an imposing round table 6.8 meters in diameter. The monstrous piece of furniture was specially made in a Moscow factory and brought to Potsdam. Quietly, almost casually, Stalin begins to speak. Instantaneously, all other conversation stops. Stalin opens the first meeting with a strange intimacy, as if only he, Churchill, and Truman were in the room, and promptly offers Truman the chairmanship. This is a clever move, as it puts the US president in the position of mediator between the Soviet Union and England. From an American perspective, this is a dilemma, and Truman's diplomats quickly gain the impression that Churchill has not prepared adequately for the conference. "Several times matters came up which revealed that he didn't seem to know what was happening," one member of the US delegation will later recall.[43]

The talks that now commence between the three powers are about nothing less than a new post-war order for Europe and the world. While the war against Japan continues in the Pacific, numerous nations in Eastern Europe—including Czechoslovakia, Hungary and Poland, the Baltic countries, and almost the entire Balkans—find themselves in the Soviet sphere of influence. The challenges could hardly be greater. First, the three powers need to agree on a common occupation policy for Germany. Territorial issues are also on the agenda. Having annexed large areas of eastern Poland, Stalin now supports Polish demands for territorial compensation in the west at Germany's expense. Lastly, a decision must be reached on what economic and financial compensation Germany will be made to pay.

The three foreign ministers—James Francis Byrnes, Anthony Eden, and Vyacheslav Molotov—usually meet in the morning to discuss the controversial points and set the agenda for the Big Three's afternoon plenary sessions. At the same time, various subcommittees are at work on less important issues, drafting texts and protocols and preparing communiqués.

This all proves tedious business, and Truman almost loses patience several times, especially whenever someone launches into a long-winded monologue. "I'm not," he writes in his diary, "going to stay around this terrible place all summer just to listen to speeches."[44]

V

On the afternoon of July 17, Secretary of War Stimson approaches Churchill in his "abode" and asks to speak with him briefly. It's about the Manhattan Project. Stimson hands the prime minister a sheet of paper with the words "Babies satisfactorily born." Churchill is, of course, in the know about American and British scientists' joint work on the Manhattan Project. No explanation is necessary, but Stimson still solemnly declares: "It means," he said, "that the experiment in the New Mexican desert has come off. The atomic bomb is a reality."[45]

Next day, Truman seeks out the British prime minister in his villa on Griebnitzsee. Churchill escorts his guest into the garden, where soldiers of the Scots Guards march up to be inspected by the US president. A military band plays "The Star-Spangled Banner," then Churchill and Truman retire to a private lunch.

"At any rate, there never was a moment's discussion as to whether the atomic bomb should be used or not," Churchill will later recall. "To avert a vast, indefinite butchery, to bring the war to an end, to give peace to the world, to lay healing hands upon its tortured peoples by a manifestation of overwhelming power at the cost of a few explosions, seemed, after all our toils and perils, a miracle of deliverance."[46]

The two statesmen agree that Stalin must be informed about the bomb in the near future, especially as the Soviets had promised to enter the war against Japan alongside

Harry S. Truman, Secretary of State James Byrnes, and Chief of Staff William Leahy (from left to right in the back seat of the car) inspect the ruins of Hitler's Reich Chancellery in Berlin in mid-July 1945.

the Americans and the British. Is that even necessary under the changed circumstances? "Believe Japs will fold up before Russia comes in," Truman confides in his diary. "I am sure they will when Manhattan appears over their homeland."[47]

V

Some six hundred kilometers from Potsdam, Richard Strauss is immersed in the study of a multivolume work of history. Friedrich von Raumer's *History of the Hohenstaufen Dynasty* is a good century old, but it's still able to captivate the composer. After reading it, Strauss understands that world history is nothing but serial stupidity, malice, murder, and destruction. He is particularly dismayed by the popes and the Catholic clergy, whose actions surpass even the shameful deeds of rulers and the nobility. But Strauss isn't done thinking about Adolf Hitler either. On July 19, he writes: "Only a criminal, an ignoramus, an uneducated fool of this magnitude could have been capable of destroying this apparently so powerful empire, inhabited by the most capable, educated people, supported by the greatest military might, so thoroughly that it must now be cured once and for all (together with like-minded Italy) of imperialist plans and must now see itself in the appointed role that it alone can and always will occupy in the world. Central Europe is the center of culture, and Germany is the heart of the world!"[48]

V

A series of festive banquets begins at Griebnitzsee. These private gatherings are intended to help Truman, Churchill, and Stalin get to know each other better and build trust. Truman kicked things off on July 19 by inviting the British and Soviet delegations to a dinner on the veranda of his villa overlooking the lake. "Had Churchill on my right, Stalin on my left," Truman writes to his wife, Bess. "We toasted the British king, the Soviet President, the U.S. President, the two honor guests, the foreign ministers, one at a time, etc. etc. ad lib."[49] At one point, Churchill raises his glass and toasts "The Leader of the British opposition—whoever he may be!"[50] Clement Attlee doesn't say a word.

After the meal, a grand piano is pushed out onto the veranda, and Sergeant Eugene List performs works by Frédéric Chopin, Carl Maria von Weber, and Franz Schubert. Born in Philadelphia to Ukrainian parents, the twenty-seven-year-old pianist is regarded as one of the most promising talents of his generation. Truman instructed him to practice nothing but Chopin for a week since Stalin is particularly fond of the Polish composer's music. After List has finished Chopin's Waltz in A minor op. 42, Stalin rises, visibly moved, and approaches the young man to toast his health. The sergeant is as white as a sheet. He doesn't quite know what is happening. Meanwhile, Churchill, who doesn't care much for serious music, sits bored in his armchair puffing on a cigar that must be a good twenty centimeters long. But noticing Stalin's enthusiasm and not wanting to play second fiddle, he also toasts List. Someone present requests that Truman, who has a reputation as a passionate amateur pianist, play something. The US president doesn't have to be asked twice, announcing that he will perform the famous minuet by Polish composer Ignacy Jan Paderewski. This little piece, written in 1887, is part of the unpretentious repertoire that young high society ladies would perform at the turn of the century. Perhaps that's why it's so popular.

"Ah yes," Stalin comments with a smile after the president has finished, "music's an excellent thing—it drives out the beast in man."[51]

V

"Two roadblocks in Wannsee on July 21," the Duhns write in their diary. "Churchill just drives through them." World history can sometimes bring minor irritations. To make matters worse, Annemarie feels unwell, something her husband, Johann, puts down to poor nutrition. They hadn't had any meat for a good three months and, apart from a little butter, no fat either. "But she's probably suffering from 'Volhynia fever,' an acute intestinal disease brought here by the Russians and spread by the Russian shit lying around everywhere and the numerous flies."[52]

V

On the evening of July 21, it's Joseph Stalin's turn to play the host. "Started," Truman writes to his wife, "with caviar and vodka and mare's milk butter, then smoked herring, then white fish and vegetables, then venison and vegetables, then duck and chicken, and finally two desserts, ice cream and strawberries, and a wind-up of sliced watermelon."[53] White wine, red wine, champagne, and cognac are served in large quantities, and every few minutes a member of the Soviet delegation stands up and makes a toast to someone else. Truman quickly realizes that he'll be drunk in no time if he empties the glasses at this pace. So he only pretends to drink, merely wetting his lips. The dinner is followed by music, and Stalin does everything he can to impress the American president. He has had his best pianists, Emil Gilels and Vladimir Sofronitsky, flown in especially for the occasion. And as if that weren't enough, he presents two outstanding violinists "who made up in musical ability what they lacked in looks," as Truman's chief of staff William D. Leahy recalls. "The president and I estimated that they weighed about 200 pounds each."[54]

Churchill doesn't enjoy the Soviet delegation's party either. The countless toasts and the never-ending musical performances are trying his patience; indeed, he is bored to death. At one point, he stands up, leans over to Truman and whispers in his ear: "When are you going home?" But unlike Churchill, the US president is in high spirits: "What's the matter? This is excellent music and I'm having a fine time. I'm going to stay until our host indicates the entertainment is over."[55] When Stalin finally calls an end to the festivities, and the guests leave his villa, the prime minister whispers that he intends to pay Truman and Stalin back for this.

V

"At Hagen I had seen a good deal of damage," notes Stephen Spender in his diary in July. "But it was in Cologne that I realized what total destruction meant."[56] Just 113 buildings in the old town—only 2 percent—survived the war, and of the rest, the things standing are the external walls, reaching to the sky like imploring hands. The once-so-proud city with its many Romanesque churches, whose towers dominated the skyline, its mighty bridges over the Rhine, its opera, theaters, cinemas, restaurants, and stores . . . the heart of the Rhineland is no longer beating. It reminds Stephen of a rotting and stinking carcass.

The thirty-six-year-old is a writer from London. In 1929, in his early twenties, he escaped stifling bourgeoisie in Great Britain, settling first in Hamburg and two years later in Berlin, where he became close friends with fellow authors W. H. Auden and Christopher Isherwood. The three writers felt magically attracted to Berlin at the time—by the city's size, pace, and, above all, gay scene. "It all comes down to sex," Stephen will recall in a novel years later. "It's a city with no virgins. Not even the kittens and puppies are virgins," while for Isherwood "Berlin meant boys."[57] Everything seemed possible. Everything was possible. Since those days a lot has changed. Stephen is twice married: first to a poet and then, after his divorce, to a concert pianist. But that's another story.

Spender left Berlin at the beginning of the Nazi regime and has now returned as a British cultural officer to his former adopted country, where he is to help restore state authority in Germany. In Cologne today—the date is July 21—Stephen wants to pay a visit to the influential Catholic dean of the city, Robert Grosche. Having miraculously survived the bombing unscathed, his house looks alien amidst all the rubble. Stephen rings the bell. "You are an Englishman," a pious-looking lady says to him, inviting him in. The dean is not at home, she adds. Her face reminds Stephen of a squashed bread roll. "Oh, perhaps you are sent by God to help us!" Stephen furrows his brow and looks at the woman quizzically.

"My name is Fraulein Dr. Fuhlsamer," she introduces herself. "Headmistress of the Girls' School at D."[58] Her nephew Rudi Bach is dying in a hospital in Bonn, she adds. His heart! Rudi is still a child, she complains in a voice full of pain, the Almighty can't want that! Before Stephen can say anything, Miss Fuhlsamer shows him a doctor's certificate stating that Rudi's life can only be saved by penicillin. But an English major brusquely informed her, the aunt, that this medication is not available to Germans. Stephen nods sympathetically, takes a piece of paper from his pocket, jots down a few sentences and tells her to take the note to the

Bonn city commander. Perhaps it will help. Miss Fuhlsamer gazes ecstatically up at the heavens, looking for a moment like a saintly figure painted by Jusepe de Ribera. Stephen is a gift from God, she says jubilantly, and gives him a copy of her book on Catholic women in art to express her gratitude.

After Stephen leaves the dean's house, he makes his way on a wide beltway, the Kaiser-Wilhelm-Ring, to an office building being used as a makeshift town hall. He's met there by the mayor of Cologne and soon to be the first chancellor of democratic West Germany, Konrad Adenauer. Adenauer has held the office of mayor previously, until 1933, but was deposed by the National Socialists, whom he publicly opposed. Recently—on May 4—the Americans reappointed the sixty-nine-year-old politician as the head of the city government.

"You could not have come at a more suitable moment," says Adenauer by way of a greeting.[59] He issued orders to rebuild Cologne—no mean feat. Stephen is surprised at how young and lively Adenauer is, although he also finds his host's outward appearance rather forgettable. "He has an energetic, though somewhat insignificant appearance: a long lean oval face, almost no hair, small blue active eyes, a little button nose and a reddish complexion."[60] In impeccable Rhenish singsong and with a self-confidence that brooks no questioning, Adenauer explains his plans. First he wants to build a ring of new satellite towns around the old center, then demolish the ruins in the middle and rebuild the houses in modern style. The creation of new cultural life, however, is just as important. "There is a hunger and thirst now for spiritual values in Germany," he stresses.[61] While Adenauer speaks about wanting the best schools, theaters, and newspapers, the best university, the best opera, and the best music and art in general for his beloved Cologne, Stephen's eyes wander past Adenauer's bald pate out the window behind him. Against the backdrop of the massive mountains of rubble outside, the new mayor's remarks seem like the daydreams of a naïve idealist. Then their time is up, and Adenauer shows his guest to the door. As if sensing Spender's skepticism, he says in farewell: "The imagination has to be provided for."[62]

Back in Potsdam, Churchill's day of revenge has arrived. On July 23, he invites the American and Soviet delegations to a dinner featuring a menu only an English chef could dream up: cold clear soup, hot turtle soup, roast sole, roast chicken, boiled new potatoes, peas, cold ham, lettuce, fruit salad, ice cream, and Scottish woodcock. Instead of serious music, the prime minister has enlisted the Royal Air Force band to play popular marches and tunes throughout the evening. At an advanced hour, Churchill's personal physician, Lord Moran, sees Stalin suddenly stand up and walk around the enormous table with his menu card collecting autographs. After a while, each member of Stalin's party follows the Generalissimo's example and asks the other guests to sign their names.

The "Big Three"—Josef Stalin, Harry S. Truman, and Winston Churchill—negotiate a new European postwar order in Potsdam. When the result of the British House of Commons election is announced at the end of July, Churchill is forced to step down and Clement Attlee takes over as the new prime minister. "Mr. Attlee does not look like a man who is hungry for power."

"This means signing twenty-eight menus," grumbles the host.[63] After dinner, Churchill, Truman, and Stalin pose for photographers on the villa's grand staircase. The American president wears a dark suit, recalling his background as the owner of a haberdashery in Kansas City, while Churchill and Stalin are dressed in military uniform.

"It was a very colorful affair, as you can see," Truman writes home to his daughter the following day. "I am enclosing you the menu and the list of guests. The menu is signed to you by J. Stalin & Winston Churchill, and the guest list is signed by all the guests."[64] When Thomas Mann in faraway California reads about the festivities in Potsdam in the press, he complains in his diary: "The three leaders in charge of reordering the world are engaged in nothing but nonsense and playing the piano."[65]

The next day begins with a pleasant task for Truman. At 10:00 a.m., he meets with Women's Army Corps telephone operators who have been flown from their battalion headquarters in Paris to run the switchboard at the "Little White House." The president thanks the young soldiers for their important work, which enables quick, secure communication between Potsdam and Washington. Truman is cordial, exchanging a few words with the women and smiling as he shakes their hands for souvenir photos. Afterward, he orders the dropping of the atomic bomb—although the actual command bears a staff officer's signature, as the US president does not sign individual military orders. He tells Secretary of War Stimson that his decision is irrevocable unless the Japanese unconditionally surrender. The earliest date for the drop will be August 3, 1945.

Truman believes that Stalin still has no inkling of the Manhattan Project. In the early evening that Tuesday, he turns to the Generalissimo and informs him as casually as possible that the United States has a "new weapon of special destructive force." Stalin displays little interest, merely replying that he hopes the Americans will make "good use of it against the Japanese."[66] That's all. "How did it go?" asks Churchill, who watched the scene from a few meters away. "He never asked a question," replies a baffled Truman.[67]

The Americans and British had not expected this. Why did the Soviet dictator react so calmly, almost serenely? What Churchill and Truman couldn't have known was that, thanks to the espionage activities of the German-born nuclear physicist Klaus Fuchs and his colleague Theodore Alvin Hall, both of whom were involved in the Manhattan Project, Stalin has known for quite some time about the development of the world's first nuclear weapon.

V

On July 24, a neighbor knocks on Else Tietze's front door, saying she accepted a long-distance letter for Mrs. Colonel, which she then hands to Else. Else thanks her and closes the door, astonished. A long-distance letter? Walking down the hall to her living room, she scrutinizes the envelope. The neighbor is right. The letter was not posted in Berlin. Else opens it and immediately recognizes her son Richard's handwriting. He's in a military hospital, he writes, and will hopefully be discharged soon. There's no need for his mother to worry. He's doing well. Traute and her husband, Hans, are in Pfarrkirchen in Bavaria and are also in good shape. "I don't need to tell you what I felt," she rejoices in her diary. "I couldn't put it into words anyway."[68] But then she realizes that the letter is dated June 28. It's almost a month old. If Richard was really going to be "discharged soon," as he wrote, shouldn't he be in Berlin by now? And if he really was well, surely he could have written again? Else's anxious waiting continues.

On July 26, the results of the House of Commons election are announced. Churchill has just arrived back in London the day before, accompanied by his daughter, Mary. Hoping that the Conservatives would win, and he could return immediately to the negotiating table in Potsdam, Churchill and his daughter left half of their things in their villa on Griebnitzsee. "Mr. Attlee does not look to me like a man who is hungry for power," Stalin had told the prime minister by way of encouragement when he left.[69] But any optimism is unfounded. "However, just before dawn I woke suddenly with a sharp stab of almost physical pain," Churchill will later recall about that morning. "A hitherto subconscious conviction that we were beaten broke forth and dominated my mind."[70] After getting out of bed at around 9:00 a.m., early by his standards, Churchill retreats to his bathroom. The prime minister is known for his eccentric habit of conducting the first governmental business of the day in the bath. A secretary sits next to the tub with pen and paper and takes dictation. As he lies in the warm water, the first preliminary election results come in. They aren't good. At around 3:00 p.m., the projected official result is announced on the radio. Labour has won 47.7 percent of the vote and 393 seats in parliament, while the Conservatives have gone down in defeat with 36.2 percent of the vote and only 197 seats. For Churchill and the Tories, this is a debacle. At 7:00 p.m. he officially resigns to King George VI at Buckingham Palace, and just thirty minutes later the monarch receives the new prime minister, Clement Attlee. "It may well be a blessing in disguise," Clementine Churchill consoles her husband that evening. "At the moment it seems quite effectively disguised," he shoots back.[71]

Two days later, on July 28, the new British delegation arrives in Potsdam. "Mr. Attlee is not so keen as old fat Winston, and Mr. Bevin looks rather rotund to be a Foreign Minister," Truman writes to his daughter. Truman liked Churchill, whereas Attlee and his chief negotiator, Ernest Bevin, strike him as sourpusses. "Attlee is an Oxford graduate and talks with that deepthroated swallowing enunciation, same as Eden does. But I understand him reasonably well. Bevin is a tough guy. He doesn't know, of course, that your dad has been dealing with that sort all his life, from building trades to coal miners. So he won't be new."[72]

And Stalin? When the Generalissimo first encounters Attlee again, he congratulates him on the election and immediately asks him if he has already set up his Gestapo.

The news of Churchill's deselection spreads like wildfire everywhere, including Berlin, where Billy Wilder is currently staying. Wilder wants to make a film about the ruins of Berlin, this crazy, decaying, starving city, and is collecting material for a screenplay. Unlike Hanuš Burger, whose documentary about the concentration camps he has just considerably cut down, Billy has an entertaining fictional film in mind. He talks to American GIs and English military policemen, to despairing university professors whose book collections have gone up in flames, to passersby on the street and to young women who offer sex for a few cigarettes. Once he visits the black market at the Reichstag and is almost tempted into selling his wristwatch. Wilder writes it all down—nothing is too insignificant. He notes the soldiers' jargon and the conversations he overhears and describes the would-be prostitutes' flirtatious overtures.

As a member of the Information Control Division, Wilder has a car and chauffeur at his disposal. The driver is

German, and as the two of them speed through the city, they talk about everything under the sun.

"This election in Great Britain—now that Attlee has defeated Churchill, what will Churchill do," the chauffeur asks the filmmaker.

"I assume he'll stay in politics," Wilder answers. "Or he'll write a book or paint."

"Won't he stage a coup?"

"I don't think so."

"You mean he doesn't want to shoot Attlee?"

"No, I don't think so."

"Are you sure?"

"Look, man, Willkie didn't attempt a coup against Roosevelt, and Dewey didn't shoot Truman."

"That's strange," replies the driver uncomprehendingly.

"Funny thing is," Wilder replies with a smile. "That's democracy."[73]

In Bonn, Stephen Spender visits little Rudi Bach in the hospital. As he enters the clinic, a group of doctors is waiting to welcome him, like an honored guest. The doctors all effusively thank him for helping get the sick boy some penicillin. Finally, he's taken to a hospital room: Rudi is lying in one bed, in the other an old man whose skin is stretched across his emaciated body like parchment. Ignoring the old man, the visitors form a semicircle around Rudi. Stephen is shocked when he sees the little boy for the first time, laid out under a starched white bedspread as though lying in state, his face pale and waxy. With the lack of emotion of which doctors alone are capable, the German physicians use some X-rays to explain Rudi's condition, dropping them on the boy's bed every time they're done with an image. Rudi is suffering from blood poisoning, and it's weakened his heart, one of the doctors states. Although his condition has improved thanks to the penicillin, his chances of recovery are still zero, the man adds, screwing up his face to underline the hopelessness of the situation. While Rudi is forced to listen to his own death sentence, Stephen grows enraged. These doctors don't care about the boy. They're obviously only interested in being able to experiment with penicillin, which is still largely unknown in Germany. He would love to say a few words of encouragement to Rudi, but the atmosphere in the completely overcrowded room doesn't allow that. Stephen promises to visit him again tomorrow and says goodbye.

When he arrives in Rudi's hospital room the next day, the boy is already feeling much better. Somewhere in Bonn, Stephen has found a book with funny drawings by Wilhelm Busch, which he gives to the little patient. Rudi immediately starts leafing through it. He too once fell very ill as a child and couldn't move his legs, Stephen tells Rudi, who is clearly delighted with his gift. But then he completely recovered and got back on his feet again. "As I said this I remembered that it was exactly this kind of thing which people said to me when I was so ill and how it had irritated me."[74]

V

In July 1945, the Berlin public transportation company BVG records a total of 36,202,000 passengers. Of them, 16,449,000 took the streetcar and 17,654,000 the subway, while 1,821,000 traveled by bus, and 278,000 used the ships that sail the lakes and rivers in and around Berlin. In 1929, the average monthly number of trips was 123,625,000.[75]

V

What color is London? If someone asked him that, Richard Brett-Smith would answer, "Brown like a deer." Strange but true, the twenty-two-year-old associates a certain color with every city he has ever visited. For him, Copenhagen is pale blue, Paris a shimmering sapphire and gold, Amsterdam the same yellow as butter, and Algiers gleaming white. Berlin is gray. The houses that survived the war, the sky above the countless ruins, the trees, the flowers along the roadside, people's clothes, even their faces—everything looks gray to him. For a little while now, Brett-Smith has been stationed in Berlin as a British soldier. He cannot remember seeing anyone with a ruddy complexion. As he sees it, even the bread that he and his comrades eat for breakfast is absolutely devoid of color.

A few days ago, Richard heard a fitting story for his depressing view of Berlin, one which made him wonder whether the inhabitants of such a completely gray city must

Soviet war correspondent Yevgeny Khaldei encounters two men wandering through the rubble on Französische Strasse in Berlin. One is wearing an armband indicating that he's blind. The other seems to be his guide. Khaldei asks them where they come from and where they're going to. They don't know.

not eventually lose their humanity altogether. "No one with whom I have discussed this story, and who lived there in those days, has refused to believe it," he later recalls. "We agree, even if it didn't happen, it easily could have happened."

One evening, the story goes, a man is walking along Knesebeckstrasse. He is tall and slim and wears an old Wehrmacht tunic, plus-fours and dark glasses. In his right hand he holds a white stick with which he taps the sidewalk in regular circular movements, and his left arm sports a yellow bandage with three black dots. The man is obviously blind. After a while, he stops and speaks to a buxom young woman who happens to cross his path.

"Excuse me, *Fräulein,* can you tell me where No.— is?" The man shows her the envelope. "I have a letter to deliver there."

"Why yes, but you're going in the wrong direction," the woman replies. "I'm walking that way. I'll show you."

"You're very kind," the blind man says. "Is it far, may I ask?"

"Quite a way. Look here, may I take your letter for you, and save you the trouble? It's not too much to do for someone who has given his country what you have given."

"Oh, that is too good of you. A thousand thanks. Yes, since Stalingrad I am rather slow. But you'll have to go right in and down the steps at this address, as part of the building was bombed out. You don't mind the trouble, are you sure?"

The letter is addressed to a shoe store. The woman takes it, says goodbye, and sets off toward the address, while the blind man continues the way he was headed. When she has gone sixty yards or so, she turns around to check on the man and sees him walking away quickly with his cane under his arm, his armband now removed. Why did he pretend to be blind? The whole thing gives her the creeps. Something is wrong. So she takes the envelope to the police, who pay a visit to the shoe store. Everything initially seems to be in order, but then the police discover a large quantity of meat in a difficult-to-access basement storeroom. Black market food, they think, but on closer inspection the meat turns out to be human flesh. At first, in the commotion that causes, nobody remembers the letter, but when a detective finally tears open the envelope, he finds a small piece of paper with a single sentence written on it: "This is the last one I shall be sending you today."[76]

V

In Potsdam, Terminal is going round in circles. "The whole difficulty is reparations," Truman confides to Bess in a letter on July 31. "Of course, the Russians are naturally looters and they have been thoroughly looted by the Germans over and over again and you can hardly blame them for their attitude." And that's not all. "The Poles are the other headache. They have moved into East Prussia and to the Oder in Prussia, and unless we are willing to go to war again, they can stay and they will stay with Bolsheviki backing."[77]

V

Berlin is shrinking. In July, there are 15,629 deaths and only 2,899 births. The statisticians speak of a negative population growth of 12,730.[78]

The Second World War is over. More than two million people in New York's Times Square celebrate the Japanese surrender.

THE BOMB

It is John's third visit to Germany. When he arrives in Berlin from Paris at the end of July, the twenty-eight-year-old reporter for media mogul William Randolph Hearst's newspaper network plans to report on events in Germany as part of a tour group led by the American Secretary of the Navy James Forrestal. "In flying over Germany," he writes in his diary, "the small towns and fields looked peaceful, but in the larger cities like Frankfurt, the buildings are merely of the sods."[1] The contrast to his last visit eight years earlier, in the summer of 1937, could hardly have been greater. At that time, John had just completed his first year at Harvard University and, together with friends, embarked on a "Grand Tour" intended to broaden his horizons and sensitize him to political events in Europe. John comes from an influential and extremely wealthy American family that places great value on education and cosmopolitanism.

The two-month trip took John and friends through France, Italy, and Austria to Germany and from there by ship via Holland and Belgium to England. "France is really quite a primitive nation," he opined.[2] He never warmed to the French, writing, "rather crowded and the distinguishing mark of the Frenchman is his cabbage breath and the fact that there are no bath-tubs."[3] Germany and its inhabitants were quite different. John went on to assert: "All the towns are very attractive, showing that the Nordic races certainly seem superior to the Latins. The Germans really are too good—it makes people gang against them for protection."[4] At the time, he was certain "that Fascism is the thing for Germany and Italy, Communism for Russia, and Democracy for America and England."[5]

Now, in the summer of 1945, John wants to understand how Hitler was able to seduce an entire nation. Although John is not a Nazi himself, he is fascinated by Hitler's defunct empire. He therefore embarks on a grim search for clues, visiting the destroyed Reich Chancellery with its "Führer's bunker" and inspecting the room where the dictator ended his life.

On August 1, John and his companions fly from Frankfurt to Salzburg, driving on from there to Berchtesgaden. They move into rooms at the Hotel Geiger, a formerly five-star establishment where Thomas Mann, Prince Max von Baden, and medical professor Ferdinand Sauerbruch all stayed. A little later, the local US Army commander invites the visitors from his home country to a reception in a luxuriously furnished building nearby. The men are told that until recently the property was used by Field Marshal Wilhelm Keitel and the Wehrmacht High Command. This isn't the whole truth. The main user was the Reich Chancellery in Berlin, which had a branch office here. Hitler had the spacious building constructed in 1937 so that he could continue to conduct government business during his stays at Obersalzberg. John is impressed by the six-hundred-meter-long bunker leading directly to the train station in Berchtesgaden. Then dinner is served. "The dinner consisted of about six courses—Rhine wines and champagne," John recalls. "After dinner, they brought out some cigars taken from Göring's armored car."[6]

The next morning, the group is driven up the Obersalzberg mountain for the conclusion and highlight of their trip to Germany. They've heard a lot about Hitler's legendary residence in the Alps, but they want to see the Berghof, the place from where the German dictator used to terrify the world, with their own eyes. John is initially disappointed. "It was completely gutted," he notes in his diary.[7] The SS had set fire to the building in the final days of the war, and Royal Air Force bombers and looters took care of the rest. In any case, there's little left of the luxury of Hitler's Alpine retreat.

John then heads to the Eagle's Nest teahouse just below the summit of the peak of the same name at an altitude of

1,800 meters. The spectacular complex was built for Hitler between 1937 and 1938, but he only used it a good ten times. It is said that the dictator found the journey up the steep road too time-consuming. The road ends in a small square, where a 124-meter-long tunnel leads through the mountain massif to an elevator that ends directly in the vestibule of the Eagle's Nest. Although the elegant interior, with its carpets, paintings, and tapestries, as well as the furniture by Hungarian designer Paul László, had also been looted, John is completely overwhelmed by the panoramic view of the Berchtesgaden Alps. "After visiting these two places, you can easily understand how that within a few years Hitler will emerge from the hatred that surrounds him now as one of the most significant figures who ever lived," John writes. "He had boundless ambition for his country which rendered him a menace to the peace of the world, but he had a mystery about him in the way he lived and in the manner of his death that will live and grow after him. He had in him the stuff of which legends are made."[8]

John's full name is John Fitzgerald Kennedy.

The Big Three's conference in Potsdam ends at midnight on August 2. "Our enemies are just taking decisions over our heads," laments Annemarie von Duhn. "It's better not to think about the fact that one was once a citizen of a free state."[9] What is actually being decided upon at Cecilienhof

Palace this midnight? The end of Germany? Hardly. Most of the agreements are deliberately vague, and the Potsdam Agreement is not a treaty in the legal sense, but merely a joint declaration of intent. The agreements will only be legally formalized at a peace conference to be convened at a later date.

The most far-reaching agreement concerns the intended recognition of the so-called Oder-Neisse line as Poland's western border, shifting Poland westward to the territorial benefit of the Soviet Union at the expense of Germany. What may sound abstract has existential consequences for millions of people. Eastern Poland will fall to Stalin and be incorporated into the Soviet Union, while East Prussia, West Pomerania, Silesia, and Gdansk become Polish. The German population still remaining there will have to flee or be expelled. In addition, the agreement lists four tasks for Germany, all of which begin with a "D": democratization, demilitarization, economic decentralization, and de-Nazification. A joint Allied Control Council is made the supreme occupation authority and granted power to exercise the highest governmental responsibilities.

"None of this is surprising," Thomas Mann writes in his diary, "but as a definitive plan it is shocking. Will it be tenable? Perhaps."[10]

Or perhaps not. Tensions between the three former allies have increased noticeably during those weeks in Potsdam. Whereas during the war there was still a need for military cooperation against the common enemy, Germany, cooperation has become much more complicated in the summer of 1945. Additionally, the British negotiating position has been significantly weakened by Churchill being voted out of office. The new prime minister, Clement Attlee, despite all his good will, has hardly been able to set the tone. And whereas Franklin D. Roosevelt had wanted to integrate the Soviet Union into a new joint world order, the United States, under Harry S. Truman, now occupies an unprecedented position as a globally dominant power thanks to the atomic bomb. Considerations for others that were opportune a short time ago no longer seem necessary.

The dividing line is by no means only between the Soviet Union and the United States. France, which did not receive a seat at the negotiating table in Potsdam but agreed in principle to the decisions made there, insists that Germany's western border be revised as well. Paris would like to see the bank of the Rhine and the Ruhr region separated from France's former enemy, but that's unacceptable to the other occupying powers. The French are aware of this but want to use the wrangling to torpedo the establishment of a German central administration, as agreed in Potsdam. Meanwhile, the Soviet Union sees the disagreement among the Western Allies as an opportunity to create a fait accompli in its own occupation zone, implementing a long-planned land reform, nationalizing key industries and reforming education in line with the Soviet model. In short, vanquished Germany has become a pawn in the hands of the Allies.

George F. Kennan saw it all coming. The forty-one-year-old diplomat, who has been working at the American embassy in Moscow for a year, doesn't trust the Soviets. Kennan views the Potsdam resolutions as absurd and impracticable, noting: "The idea of a Germany run jointly with the Russians is a chimera. The idea of both the Russians and ourselves withdrawing politely at a given date and a healthy, peaceful, stable, and friendly Germany arising out of the resulting vacuum is also a chimera. We have no choice but to lead our section of Germany—the section of which we and the British have accepted responsibility—to a form of independence so prosperous, so secure, so superior, that the East cannot threaten it."[11] The logical extension of Kennan's warning is the dividing of Germany into two states, but no one wants to hear about that so soon after the end of the Potsdam Conference.

When Truman says goodbye to Stalin at 12:40 a.m., he expresses his wish that their next meeting take place in Washington. "God willing," replies Stalin, who was schooled in a monastery, with a smile.[12] The two will never lay eyes on each other again.

One could get the impression that Truman wants to put the Potsdam Conference and its agreements behind him as quickly as possible. Such is his hurry to leave Germany. After a few hours' sleep, he sets off for the airport at 7:15 a.m.. There, he and his entourage immediately board three separate planes. At Truman's express request, no honors are paid to him in Gatow—everything is to be done very quickly. At 8:05 a.m., Lieutenant Colonel H. T. Myers throttles up the engine and the "Sacred Cow" ascends into the sky over Potsdam in no time.

V

Sometime in early August, a truck from Potsdam rattles along the main boulevard into Berlin. It stops near Steglitz district town hall, the passenger door opens and a young man jumps down from the driver's seat. He shouts something to the driver, waves farewell and then closes the door. The truck speeds off, leaving the man alone. It is already dusk. Darkness covers the ruined city like a shroud.

Richard Tietze has had a difficult time lately. After his release from the military hospital, he was initially transferred to an American POW camp but was released after a few weeks. He then struggled to make his way to Berlin from the southwestern German city of Karlsruhe via Giessen and Weimar. As much as Richard longed to return to his hometown, he feared the worst. His mother, Else, never replied to his letter. Is she even still alive?

He walks with no small trepidation from Schlossstrasse to Stubenrauchplatz, then turns right onto Holsteinische Strasse. His heart beats faster and faster with excitement. Richard realizes with relief that his parents' house is still standing. The light is on in the living room. He steps through the front door and then climbs the stairs. "Tietze" is the name on the apartment door on the second floor. He hesitates for a second, then softly knocks.

V

"To get in here," one of the soldiers tells Erika Mann, "you have to have a pass from God and someone has to verify the signature."[13] He laughs sarcastically, as if to make the visitor understand that she had better turn on her heel and disappear. She hadn't driven all night from Paris to get here, Erika counters, to be so easily brushed off. She demands to speak to Burton C. Andrus, the commander of the facility. But he also turns her down. "No good!" Andrus replies coolly, "Your mission is nowhere defined."[14] He tells her to go to the US Army headquarters in Frankfurt am Main. No sooner said than done. After some back and forth, Erika receives a certificate that, while not bearing the signature of the Almighty, has been signed by the highest military authorities. That does the trick. A few days later, when she shows the guard the letter, he lets her pass.

Erika Mann is in the small Luxembourg village of Mondorf-les-Bains, where world history is being written. The picturesque spa town in the southwest of the grand duchy, right on the border with France, is famous for its thermal springs, which promise relief for liver and gallbladder complaints, rheumatic diseases and, in particular, respiratory ailments. But thirty-nine-year-old Erika hasn't ventured into the Luxembourg provinces for her health, although that might not be a bad idea considering she's a chain smoker. Since 1943, Erika has worked for various newspapers as a war correspondent. Her travels have taken her to Egypt, Belgium, France, and Palestine, among other places. When the Western Allies landed in Normandy on June 6, 1944, she was there, and she's experienced many tight situations and risked her life more than once. But today's visit to Mondorf is something very special to her. She's been preparing for this moment for twelve long years.

Strictly shielded from the public eye, the Americans have set up an interrogation center in a luxury hotel, which bears the less-than-poetic code name "Camp Ashcan." Almost all the former Nazi bigwigs US forces have been able get their hands on have been brought here. In addition to Hermann Göring, who was transferred from Augsburg, the eighty-six inmates included government ministers in the Third Reich and high-ranking officials and generals such as Wilhelm Keitel, Karl Dönitz, Wilhelm Frick, Alfred Rosenberg, Albert Speer, Hans Frank, Fritz Sauckel, Joachim von Ribbentrop, and Julius Streicher. It is hoped that interrogating these men will provide insights both into their involvement in the crimes of Nazi Germany and its structures in general.

Erika may feel she owes it to herself, her family, and the millions of other people who suffered under National Socialism. In any case, she wants to see the criminals who brought so much suffering to the world face-to-face. "I felt my private V.E.-Day," she'll later note.[15] Erika doesn't have much time left. In a few days—on August 10—the inmates are to be transferred from Mondorf to Nuremberg. After lengthy discussions, the Allies have selected the city that once hosted the Nazi Party Rallies as the seat of the International Military Tribunal for the main perpetrators of Nazi crimes.

"Camp Ashcan" initially strikes Erika like a high-security prison. The entire area is surrounded by a four-and-a-half-meter-high barbed wire fence. There is a watchtower at every corner, each manned by two soldiers and equipped with a clearly visible machine gun. Camouflage nets and large tarpaulins hang down from trees and posts throughout the spacious grounds to prevent anyone from seeing what is going on inside the fence. While the actual building with its four stories, imposing central tower, and large terrace is certainly something to behold, the rooms themselves have little of the elegance of a luxury hotel. All the furniture has been removed and stored in a nearby monastery. Instead of comfortable beds, armchairs, leather armchairs, and stylish desks, the rooms of the camp's "guests" are furnished with a folding cot, a simple chair and a plain wooden table. And steel bars, of course. Despite the ambience, it is clear to everyone incarcerated here that the whole thing is nothing but a prison.

Hermann Göring arrived in Mondorf in May with sixteen monogrammed suitcases, a red hatbox, seven watches, precious rings, brooches, chains and medals, a gold-plated pencil, a gold cigarette case, and 81,268 Reichsmarks in cash. In Göring's heyday, no public appearance was ever deemed too pompous. "The uniform takes precedence over the office," Nazi propaganda minister Joseph Goebbels had once mockingly written of him.[16] When Göring inspected his "guest room," he was horrified and immediately demanded to see the officer in charge, John Dolibois, to whom he introduced himself as "Göring, Reichsmarschall." Dolibois later recalls: "Goering then planted his feet apart, put his hands behind his back and lodged his first complaint. He had been 'misled' by the American officers to whom he had surrendered 'voluntarily.' In Augsburg he had been told that he was going to a palatial spa and would be treated royally, as deserving the ex-commander in chief of the German Luftwaffe, a marshal of the Reich."[17] Göring is quickly disabused of such notions.

Joachim von Ribbentrop, who was captured in Hamburg, where he was hiding under a false name, cuts a figure as tragic as it is ridiculous. During his time as Reich Foreign Minister, many diplomats considered him an arrogant snob, an unlikeable busybody and a supercilious blowhard who tortured his fellow human beings with vacuous monologues. Nor did Ribbentrop, who had married the daughter of the wealthy champagne manufacturer Otto Henkell in 1920, have many friends in the uppermost leadership of the Third Reich, either. Goebbels regarded Ribbentrop as an impostor who had only acquired his "von" by having himself adopted in 1925 by a childless, aristocratic aunt—in return for a lifelong pension of 450 marks a month. "He bought his name, he married his money, and he swindled his way into office," Goebbels sneered.[18] Annelies von Ribbentrop, née Henkell, was equally unpopular. "She was an aggressive, pushy bitch," Ribbentrop's secretary Margarete Blank later remembers.[19]

In Mondorf, the once-dashing Ribbentrop spirals into self-pity and declares he wants to kill himself, whereabout his trouser belt, ties, and shoelaces are taken away to prevent him from committing suicide. He has no mirror or electricity in his room and has to hand in his razor blade after shaving in the morning. A Jewish GI from Brooklyn ensures that the rules are observed.

The most repulsive and gruesome figure among the Mondorf prisoners is undoubtedly Julius Streicher. The sixty-year-old was a Nazi from day one. He formed the Nuremberg branch of the Nazi Party in the fall of 1922, founded the weekly SS newspaper *Der Stürmer* in April 1923, took part in Hitler's Munich putsch in November 1923, and became the so-called Gauleiter (regional leader) of Franconia in 1925. Hitler liked cold-blooded and unscrupulous fanatics like Streicher, who was one of the handful of people who were allowed to address the dictator with the familiar second-person pronoun *Du*. For Hitler, Streicher was *the* embodiment of National Socialism, while for many others he was a homicidal psychopath.

Streicher's worldview can be reduced to a simple slogan: "The Jews are our misfortune!" This quote from historian Heinrich von Treitschke appeared on every front page of *Stürmer,* and the hatred it entailed ran through the paper like a basso continuo. Streicher's anti-Semitism also expressed itself in sexual obsessions. For example, he repeatedly published salacious stories about the alleged rape of young "Aryan" girls by older Jewish men. "Starving

Germans Girls in the Clutches of Horny Jew Bucks" was one particularly lurid headline.[20] The *Stürmer* also traded on reports of alleged ritual murders with titles like "Who is the Butcher of Children in Breslau?"[21] Such extreme examples of slander often left even dyed-in-the-wool National Socialists shaking their heads.

Streicher's fellow prisoners in Mondorf make no secret of their contempt for him. The first time he first appears in the dining room for dinner, the others demonstratively turn their backs on him or even leave the room. Others feel so offended by Streicher's presence that they formally request, then demand from Burton C. Andrus that they not have to eat in the same room as Streicher. This provides Andrus with a welcome opportunity to show the inmates who is in charge at Camp Ashcan. The commandant has all the men line up as if for a roll call and gives a speech about the wages of sin. Part of their punishment as Nazi criminals, he says, is precisely to have to break bread with someone like Streicher.

The prisoners' everyday lives are monotonous. When they are not being interrogated, they go for walks in the park, play chess, read, or sit on the terrace in the sun. Only Streicher fills his days with feverish activity. Like the lunatic Dr. Mabuse in Fritz Lang's famous film *The Testament of Dr. Mabuse,* released the same year the Nazis came to power, Streicher spends his days in his cell, scribbling frenetically. But whereas Mabuse writes down plans for murders and acts of terror to be carried out by his criminal organization, Streicher is spinning political delusions: "The Führer is not dead! He lives on in the creation of his godlike spirit."[22]

Arriving in Camp Ashcan, Erika Mann can't help asking herself whether she has entered a madhouse. The idea that "tout le horreur du monde" gathered under one roof makes her take several deep breaths. She is not allowed to speak to the inmates, Dolibois tells her, but he can take her from cell to cell so that she can observe the inmates. When the men find out afterward who the visitor was, most are upset. In a letter to her father Thomas, Erika relates their reactions: "Ley shouted, 'Assez!' and covered his face in hands. Rosenberg muttered, 'Pfui! To hell with this woman!'... Göring was the most agitated. If only I had introduced myself, he said, he would have explained everything, and if he had handled the Mann case, he would have handled the matter differently. A German of T.M.'s stature could certainly have been adapted to the Third Reich."[23]

Only Julius Streicher seems to have recognized Erika straight away. "Streicher was in the cell," Dolibois will recall. "He usually turned his back to the door and stood there with his feet apart. It was a characteristic pose, artificial, aggressive, a James Cagney–type posture. I opened the door and went in. When he heard my voice, he turned around. Then he saw Erika Mann standing in the doorway and knew immediately who she was. He spread his legs a little wider, crossed his arms, smiled mockingly and said: 'So, you've come to stare at all the wild animals in the zoo.' Whereupon he said,

'Then you might as well see everything!' He dropped his pants and exposed himself."[24]

What is Erika's reaction? So there we have it, she might think, "a member of the master race" and a dirty old man with a crazed look in his eyes. She flicks the ash off her cigarillo, turns around and walks on to the next room.

In recent days, Paul Tibbets may have thought back to what his father said when he learned that he wanted to become a pilot: "Well, I've sent you through school, bought you automobiles, given you money to run around with the girls, but from here on, you're on your own. If you want to go kill yourself, go ahead, I don't give a damn."[25] For as long as he could remember, the old man ranted on, there had always been a doctor in the Tibbets family. The fact that Tibbets Senior, as a wholesaler of confectionery, himself broke this rule may only have encouraged Paul in his plans. In any case, Paul Junior didn't study medicine; instead he became a pilot, joining the American military and taking part in the war against Germany in June 1942. Paul is regarded as one of the best flyers in the ranks of the Air Force, which is one of the reasons why, as a thirty-year-old, he has now been entrusted with a top-secret mission. He has assembled a crew of eleven others, three of whom—Tom Ferebee, Wyatt Duzenbury, and navigator Theodore "Dutch" Van Kirk—he has already flown missions with across Europe. Paul trusts his men, but he has kept them in the dark about what exactly they will be facing.

"You figure out what time we have to start after midnight to be over the target at 9:00 a.m.," Paul whispers to his navigator.[26] It's early afternoon on Sunday, August 5. "Dutch" Van Kirk bends over a pile of maps and calculates the expected flight time of a Boeing B-29 from Tinian, one of the Northern Mariana Islands in the eastern Philippine Sea in the Pacific Ocean, to the location of their mission. "Dutch" calculates a flying time of six-and-a-half hours. Then Paul takes a bucket of paint and writes the words "Enola Gay" on the metal below the cockpit of the B-29. It's his mother's name—unlike his father, she always supported him becoming a pilot. Finally, a bomb is loaded on board. Its designers have nicknamed it "Little Boy," a reference to the boyish, slender director of the atomic bomb program, Robert Oppenheimer.

At 2:45 the next morning, the "Enola Gay" takes off, accompanied by other aircraft to scout the weather conditions and the strength of the air defenses over the target. At some point during the flight, Paul Tibbets goes to the back of the plane and addresses his crew.

"You know what we're doing today?" he asks the men with a grave face.

"Well, yeah, we're going on a bombing mission," says a soldier named Bob.

"Yeah, we're going on a bombing mission, but it's a little bit special."

"Colonel, we wouldn't be playing with atoms today, would we?"

"Bob, you've got it just exactly right."[27]

V

It's 9:05 a.m. The *Enola Gay* is flying at an altitude of 31,060 feet and a speed of two hundred miles per hour when the city of Hiroshima appears before Paul's eyes. He recognizes the wide, flat delta of the Ōta River, which divides the city into several small islands. The tide is high so the river's arms, which are lined with cherry trees, are completely full of water. To the north and northwest, a few hills above the city plain form a gently outlined silhouette. From Paul's cockpit, the world down there looks peaceful and idyllic.

Michihiko Hachiya has only just gotten home a few minutes ago from a night shift as an air-raid warden at his clinic. The forty-two-year-old physician is completely exhausted and lies down on his hard living room floor to relax when Tom Ferebee opens the bomb bay of the *Enola Gay* at 9:15 a.m., releasing its payload. Forty-four seconds later the apocalypse begins for Hiroshima's two hundred forty-five thousand inhabitants.

"Suddenly, a strong flash of light startled me—and then another," recalls Michihiko. "All over the right side of my body I was cut and bleeding. A large splinter was protruding from a mangled wound in my thigh, and something warm trickled into my mouth. My cheek was torn, I discovered as I felt it gingerly, with the lower lip laid wide open. Embedded in my neck was a sizable fragment of glass which I matter-of-factly dislodged, and with the detachment of one stunned and shocked I studied it and my blood-stained hand."[28]

Michihiko and his wife, Yaeko-san, are lucky enough to survive the disaster, having been a kilometer-and-a-half from ground zero. People who are closer literally evaporate. Within a second, the shock wave from the detonation destroys 80 percent of the city center, killing instantly seventy thousand to eighty thousand people. There are hellish scenes, such as when the glaring light of the explosion burns the outline of a man sitting on a stone bench into the solid rock, while nothing remains of him.

Meanwhile Harry S. Truman is on board the cruiser USS *Augusta* on his way back to the United States. The president spends the early morning on deck in calm seas, enjoying the sun and listening to a concert by the ship's band, then works on some important papers in his cabin until lunch. Shortly before noon, Truman is having lunch with the crew when he receives a short message, marked as top priority, from the Department of the Navy. It informs him that the Air Force has dropped an atomic bomb on Hiroshima, and it has been a complete success. Truman is electrified.

"This is the greatest thing in history," he says to the sailors around him, visibly moved. "It's time for us to get home."[29] A short time later, the White House publishes a presidential press release, drafted in advance in Potsdam, that contains an ominous threat directed at the Japanese government: "If they do not now accept our terms they may expect a rain of ruin from the air, the like of which has never been seen on this earth."[30]

V

How often might Kantarō Suzuki have regretted in recent weeks that he, as an old man of seventy-seven, has not been spared this. Suzuki hasn't been in the best of health since surviving an assassination attempt in 1936. At the time, mutinous army officers shot him four times, even putting a bullet between his eyes. Miraculously, he survived. The retired admiral had certainly imagined a different retirement, but when Emperor Hirohito asked him to take over as Japanese prime minister in April, he obeyed, as he had learned to do as a soldier.

In the early morning of August 9, Suzuki no longer knows what to do. Having relied on the mediation of the Soviet Union to end the war with the United States, he now learns that Soviet Foreign Minister Molotov declared war on Japan in a conversation with the latter's ambassador in the Kremlin the previous evening. Soviet troops have already marched into Japanese-occupied Manchuria. What the Japanese don't know is that Stalin is acting on a secret agreement that he, Roosevelt, and Churchill had concluded at the Yalta Conference in February 1945. It obliged the Soviet Union to enter the war against Japan two to three months after the German surrender, and Stalin has had over a million soldiers transferred from Europe to the Far East since May 9.

The news of the Soviet offensive has caught Suzuki completely off guard, and he immediately calls an emergency meeting of the War Cabinet, consisting of Foreign Minister Shigenori Tōgō, War Minister Korechika Anami, Navy Minister Mitsumasa Yonai, and two other military officers. What should they do? The War Cabinet can only make decisions unanimously, but there's no consensus at all. Suzuki, Tōgō, and Yonai argue in favor of starting negotiations with the United States, likely resulting in surrender. Anami refuses, and his two military colleagues counter with a proposal containing conditions that President Truman is never going to accept.

While the six cabinet members argue bitterly about whether, in the event they surrender, foreign troops should be allowed to occupy Japan, whether Japanese troops should voluntarily lay down their arms, and whether war crimes trials should only be allowed in domestic Japanese courts, an American B-29 bomber approaches the Japanese coastal town of Kokura, which lies under thick clouds. Major Charles W. Sweeney, the pilot of the plane, makes three attempts to carry out his mission before deciding to head for Nagasaki, some two hundred kilometers away. At 11:02 a.m., the under carriage of the plane opens and a plutonium bomb with the force of twenty-two-thousand tons of TNT hurtles toward the ground. At a height of around 470 meters above the ground, "Fat Boy," as the soldiers have christened this monster, explodes. The air heats up to more than three thousand degrees. Anyone standing anywhere near is instantly vaporized. Even two kilometers away, people's clothing catches fire. A few minutes after the explosion, thirty thousand city inhabitants are dead: vaporized, crushed by debris, consumed by the blaze.

As this is going on, the war cabinet's discussions continue. But there's no breaking the impasse.

Late in the evening of August 9, Suzuki informs Hirohito that he's been unable to broker an agreement in the War Cabinet. The members are at complete loggerheads. The Japanese prime minister knows no other way out than to ask the emperor to end the stalemate. This is remarkable since Hirohito, despite his extensive powers, does not usually interfere in day-to-day politics. But now he puts his foot down and calls on his government to initiate a surrender, on the condition that the monarchy endures and the position of the emperor—i.e. his own—remains untouched.

When the Americans learn of this declaration of intent on August 10, they're initially perplexed. "Were we to treat this message from Tokyo as an acceptance of the Potsdam Declaration?" Truman will later recall thinking. "There had been many in this country who felt that the Emperor was an integral part of that Japanese system which we were pledged to destroy. Could we retain the Emperor and yet expect to eliminate the warlike spirit in Japan?"[31] It's a good question.

V

Seventeen-year-old prisoner of war Alfred Misselhorn is still in Camp Garibaldi in Rennes. In addition to the work that the young people have to perform there, every day they also receive a few hours of schooling. On August 11, an incident occurs at lunch. Alfred reports in his diary: "One of the two night workers lost his cool and threw soup at the other with a spoon. There was a commotion. The whole barrack was in an uproar. Our teachers prevented the worst, and a court was convened to decide on a punishment. They agreed to twenty lashes on the offender's buttocks, and from then on the night workers had to share their rations evenly with the whole barracks. The delinquent survived the punishment."[32]

V

On August 12, 1945, 2,807,405 people are living in Berlin. That's 1.5 million fewer than in May 1939. Seventy percent of Berliners are Protestant, almost 11 percent are Roman Catholics, and 6,556 are Jewish—0.2 percent of Berlin's total population.[33]

V

There is disagreement in Washington about how to deal with the Japanese offer of surrender. Secretary of War Stimson advises against overthrowing the emperor, while Secretary of State Byrnes argues in favor of it. After some back and forth, a compromise is finally formulated, according to which the final form of government in Japan is to be determined by the freely expressed will of the Japanese people. This is well-intentioned, but now it reignites the discussions in Tokyo itself. Fifty-eight-year-old War Minister Anami once again proves a fanatic, firmly rejecting surrender and instead calling upon his army to prepare for a large-scale battle on the Japanese mainland. Somehow, he thinks, Japan can inflict such heavy losses on the Allies that it will be able to avoid surrendering.

On the morning of August 14, still waiting for an official response, Truman orders the resumption of conventional air strikes. In the course of that day, a Tuesday, more than one thousand B-29 bombers fly the largest one-day air raid of the war on Japanese cities. Japan's last operating oil refinery is also hit. The country is finished. In the evening, Hirohito informs his military that he will accept the American terms in full. His decision is irrevocable, and he will address the Japanese people with a formal declaration. The War Cabinet unanimously signs the declaration of surrender.

War Minister Anami and the two colleagues who have so far adamantly refused to surrender, cannot disobey the emperor. Anami knows what he must do next. At around 1:00 a.m. that night, he receives his brother-in-law and closest confidant Masahiko Takeshita. The minister has a large bottle of sake, two cups, and some cheese brought. The men drink. He is duty-bound to obey the emperor, Anami explains, but no one can force him to witness the surrender. At around four o'clock, the hour of *seppuku* arrives: a form of suicide that has existed since the mid-twelfth century, in which a man seeks to restore his honor. This ritual of self-disembowelment has been banned in Japan since 1868 but is still occasionally practiced. Anami puts on a loose white shirt that he once received as a gift from Hirohito. He kneels down in the traditional Japanese seiza posture, squatting on his heels. In front of him is a tantō, a fighting sword in an elaborately lacquered sheath. Takeshita acts as his second. Anami pulls the tantō out of its sheath with grave piety and plunges it into his stomach, which he immediately slashes from left to right about six centimeters below the navel before wrenching the blade upward. His intestines fall out immediately, but Anami is still conscious. Holding the sword in his right hand, he feels for his carotid artery with his left. Takeshita asks him if he needs help, but Anami shakes his head. With his final ounce of strength, he rams the tantō into his neck.

Hirohito is the 124th ruler on the Chrysanthemum Throne. According to the constitution of the Empire of Greater Japan, the emperor is divinely appointed, and his person is sacred and inviolable. A god does not normally speak to his subjects—at least not over the radio. Most Japanese have never heard the voice of their ruler, so what happens on the afternoon of August 15 is nothing less than the earthly incarnation of a god. Loudspeakers crackle, then a man says in a high, almost monotonous voice: "Although everyone has done their best [. . .], the course with the war has not exactly taken a turn for the better and the international situation is not in our favor. Moreover, the enemy has recently begun to use a cruel bomb, he has often shed the blood of innocents and the extent of destruction is indeed immeasurable. Should we continue the fight, it would ultimately bring not only the destruction of our people, but also the destruction of human civilization."[34]

It's the forty-four-year-old Hirohito. His speech was recorded the night before. At the last minute, fanatic soldiers try to prevent it from being broadcast, but the coup attempt fails. Only educated Japanese are able to understand the convoluted court Japanese the emperor uses, but most people in the country immediately get the gist of what their emperor is telling them just six days after Nagasaki. Japan is laying down its arms.

"At 7.00 p.m., the White House correspondents gathered in my office," Truman will recall.[35] Just like three months earlier, when the US president announced Germany's surrender, the Oval Office is bursting at the seams. In addition to Truman, Bess, and most of the cabinet, former Secretary of State Cordell Hull is present as a guest of honor. Just a few weeks previously—on June 26—the seventy-three-year-old diplomat signed the United Nations Charter, which he had been instrumental in negotiating. The mood of those present is relaxed. Jokes are made. Then Truman takes to his feet, silencing the conversations, and reads out a short statement saying that Japan has surrendered unconditionally. "Arrangements are now being made for the formal signing of the surrender terms at the earliest possible moment," Truman announces.[36] A few minutes later, when Truman finishes speaking, the journalists sprint out of the Oval Office. A few shout out congratulations to the US president, but most just want to get to a phone as quickly as possible to pass on the good news to their editors.

Over the next few hours, more than two million people gather in Times Square in front of the *New York Times* building to celebrate. The bars in the area are packed to the rafters, people are dancing on the tables and strangers are hugging each other in the streets. The Big Apple is gripped by a veritable frenzy of joy.

Alfred Eisenstaedt pushes his way through the crowds of revelers. The forty-six-year-old, who hails from Pomerania but had to leave Germany because of his Jewish ancestry, has been living for a good ten years in the United States, where he has been able to make a name for himself as a photographer.

In New York's Times Square, German-born photographer Alfred Eisenstaedt notices a sailor coming toward him. "He was grabbing every female he could find and kissing them all—young girls and old ladies alike."

Alfred hopes to get a few good shots he can sell to newspapers and magazines. A Leica IIIa dangles around his neck. He swears by the 35mm camera, which has the advantage of being small and inconspicuous. People often don't even notice when he takes their picture. But this evening, it's as though he were cursed. Random people are constantly intruding in front of his lens or blocking out lines of sight that have just opened up. What he needs now is luck, lots of it, and a direct connection between his brain and his fingertips.

Alfred lets his gaze wander and spots a young sailor coming his way. "He was grabbing every female he could find and kissing them all—young girls and old ladies alike," the photographer later remembers. "Then I noticed the nurse standing in that enormous crowd. I focused on her, and just as I had hoped, the sailor came along, grabbed the nurse, and bent down to kiss her." At this moment, Alfred pulls the trigger, taking one of the most famous photos of all time. "Luck," he'll admit. "But you do have to keep your eyes open, too!"[37]

V

From the diary of Alfred Misselhorn. Sunday, August 19: "1/6 bread, broth, 1 liter of barley soup, carrots and meat, ½ liter of semolina flour soup, 1/8 bread, tea. Red Cross supplies from German depots were distributed today. 15 cigarettes, ½ packet of tobacco, sweets and cookies. A great joy. The items are from 1944 and have been inspected (visually)."[38]

V

Since the concert at the end of May, Leo Borchard has already made twenty further appearances with the Berliner Philharmonic. They have played at the Titania-Palast, the Haus des Rundfunks, and the Haus am Waldsee, a stately villa in the Zehlendorf district. The Philharmonic and Leo get along so well that at the beginning of June the forty-six-year-old was entrusted with leading the orchestra until further notice. The musicians are grateful to have an experienced conductor in their "zero hour," since Wilhelm Furtwängler, the previous chief conductor, is considered politically compromised and has been banned from working by the Americans.

As the new head of the Philharmonic, Leo is often invited to social occasions by representatives of the Allied occupying powers. August 23 is one of them. At around 7:00 p.m., he and Ruth are picked up by a car and chauffeured to a villa in the Grunewald forest. The host is a British officer, who is said to be an art lover. The guests sink back into heavy leather armchairs and are served whiskey and meat sandwiches on white bread. Leo and Ruth enjoy being able to eat their fill for a change. They talk about Johann Sebastian Bach, whose music the host loves, Germany, and the future. When Ruth looks at her watch at some point, she's startled. Night curfew begins in fifteen minutes. Another guest, a British colonel, offers the couple a quick ride home in his private car. It's not too far from Grunewald to Hünensteig Street, where Leo and

Ruth live. With any luck, they should be home by the time curfew begins at eleven.

The colonel is at the wheel, with Leo beside him and Ruth in the back seat. The two men are talking animatedly about Bach's *Brandenburg Concertos* as they pass the checkpoint between the British and American sectors on Kaiserplatz square. Ruth recognizes three shadows—presumably American soldiers—waving flashlights in the darkness of the railroad underpass. Are the GIs looking for a lift? Or do they want the car to stop? The driver and Leo are engrossed in their conversation and take no notice.

"Next time I'll give you Bach," Leo is saying to the colonel when Ruth suddenly hears a strange noise—as if someone is throwing gravel against the body of the car.[39] There's a bang. Several shots perforate the car. The sedan comes to a halt about ten meters beyond the tunnel.

"Leo!" Ruth cries. "Is something wrong?" But Leo doesn't answer. He's slumped in his seat. Ruth yanks open the door and sees her boyfriend bleeding. "Help!" she screams at the top of her lungs. "He's bleeding to death..." The colonel, who, like Ruth, has remained uninjured, goes around to the passenger side and looks at Leo's lifeless body. "I'm afraid...," he says, his voice breaking. "I'm afraid...it's too late..."[40]

What on earth has happened? The night before, there had been one of the frequent gunfights between Americans and Russians. The American occupying forces have issued an order for all cars approaching a checkpoint to stop. If a car does not comply, GIs are to open fire. The soldiers didn't recognize the British license plate on the colonel's car in the dark. They probably assumed that the occupants were Russian and opened fire.

For Ruth Andreas-Friedrich, this night is like a never-ending nightmare. Accompanied by the colonel, she wanders through the streets, unable to think straight. Eventually she arrives at home. She slowly climbs the stairs and then wakes Karin and her other friends in the apartment. "Leo's dead," she says apathetically. "Get up and get dressed. You can't be in your pajamas when Leo has died."[41]

V

In cities like Berlin, Hamburg, and Munich, women can occasionally be seen forming human chains of twenty or more. Standing half a meter apart, they pass metal buckets to each other, containing rubble, stones, and debris from past bombings, which now needs to be removed. This is how the inner cities are to be cleared of the ruins of the war. The women aren't working voluntarily. Many are former Nazis whom the Allies have conscripted as a form of punishment, while others signed up for such work out of sheer necessity, as those who do the heavy-clearing work are entitled to extra food rations. "I should have joined the party," many in Berlin complain. "Then I'd have something to eat now!"[42] In years to come, people will romanticize the efforts of the "rubble women," as they become known colloquially. In reality,

In many German cities, women are involved in clearing the war debris. Quite a few are conscripted by the Allies, while others volunteer because those who do heavy clearing work receive better food rations.

the "female construction assistants," as they are officially referred to in German, are the exception to the rule. In 1945 Berlin, for instance, less than 5 percent of the female population of working age is employed as "rubble women." Most of the clearance work is carried out by professional companies with heavy equipment.

When Billy Wilder passes a column of "rubble women" in Berlin in August, he stops his military jeep, leaps out of the car and approaches one of them, who is only too eager to talk.

"I'm so glad you Americans have finally arrived..."

"Why's that?" Billy interrupts.

"Because you're going to help us fix the gas."

"That we will," Billy replies, nodding.

"That's the only thing my mother and I are waiting for..."

"I suppose it will be nice to have a hot meal again."

"Not for cooking..."

A pause ensues, during which the two look at each other. Billy suspects what the woman is suggesting, but he hopes she won't say it explicitly.

"We would turn the oven on. But not light it. You understand? We'd just inhale deeply."

"Why do you say that?" asks the bewildered filmmaker.

"Why?" the woman replies reproachfully. "Because we Germans no longer have anything worth living for."

Billy shakes his head. "If you mean a life devoted to Hitler, I think you're right."[43]

V

If you're celebrating something in Los Angeles these days, you simply must get a table at Romanoff's. The restaurant on North Rodeo Drive in Beverly Hills is one of the most elegant and expensive establishments in the city, frequented by movie stars like David Niven, Humphrey Bogart, and Gregory Peck, musicians such as Cole Porter, Artur Rubinstein, and Lauritz Melchior, the influential journalist Elsa Maxwell and Gretchen Donahue from the Woolworth dynasty. Now and again, you can also spot German and Austrian emigrees such as Thomas Mann, who had a weakness for luxury, and Alma Mahler-Werfel, who loves inviting her friends here. The menu at Romanoff's includes eggs Benedict, filet mignon, frog legs, lobster, and much more. The "Strawberries Romanoff"—strawberries in Grand Marnier, mixed with whipped cream and creamy ice cream—are famous near and far.

When you enter the restaurant, you will often see an elegantly dressed man with neatly parted hair and an Adolphe Menjou moustache sitting at one of the round tables, cutting up a lobster. To his left and right sit two powerful bulldogs, with which the man shares the food on white porcelain plates. They're called Confucius and Socrates, and they greedily lick up their master's gift. The man's name is Prince Michael Dimitri Alexandrovich Obolensky-Romanoff. He's a nephew of Tsar Nicholas II—at least that's what he claims. In earlier years, His Imperial Highness also pretended to be

Harry F. Gerguson is the owner Romanoff's, the most fashionable restaurant in Los Angeles. Every day, he takes lunch there with his bulldogs Confucius and Socrates.

the son of the British Prime Minister William Gladstone, who died in 1898, claimed to have killed Rasputin or, somewhat less exotically, passed himself off as the son of William Rockefeller, William K. Vanderbilt, or some other business magnate.

His real name is Hershel Geguzin. He was born in Lithuania and fled as a child with his parents from anti-Semitic pogroms in his home country to New York City, where he changed his name to Harry F. Gerguson. What followed was a checkered career featuring numerous petty crimes, but Harry has always somehow managed to pull his head out of the noose, if need be, by inventing some wild new story, if things got too hot. In 1941, "Mike Romanoff" opened his eponymous restaurant. None who patronizes the place seriously believes that Harry actually is a Romanoff prince, but that doesn't matter. Thanks to his constant antics, the ever-eager tabloid press had long made him a legend. Nor has his success as a restauranteur noticeably diminished the arrogance that has always been a major part of his charm. He snubs most of his patrons and is particularly contemptuous of empty blowhards, for whom he, as a master impostor, has an unerring sense.

Niven will later recall how the headwaiter once approached Harry's table, where he was dining with his dogs. The waiter bowed his head respectfully and whispered to the boss: "'We must find room for this party, Mr. Romanoff—they're very important... eight of them.'

"'Who are they?' demanded Mike.

"'Oil men from Texas and society people from Pasadena—very rich.'

"'Peasants,' said His Imperial Highness. 'Fuck 'em.'"[44]

V

Alma Mahler-Werfel and her husband Franz are in an upbeat mood. It's August 25, and after more than two years of work, Werfel's new novel, *Star of the Unborn,* is finally done. The couple are expecting a visit that evening from conductor Bruno Walter and his daughter Lotte, who purchased the neighboring property on North Bedford Drive only a few weeks ago, to toast the new book together. Afterward, they plan to dine at Romanoff's, where Alma has reserved a table. The Walters arrive a little bit early. While Alma and Franz get dressed, Walter plays a few bars from Smetana's opera *The Bartered Bride* on Alma's Steinway grand piano. When Werfel recognizes the melodies, which he has known since childhood, he immediately comes out of his room, hums along with them and performs a few bashful dance steps. That's astonishing. The fifty-four-year-old Werfel has a heart condition and suffered his latest mild heart attack just a week before. But he recovered quickly, and despite Alma's understandably great concern for her husband, this promises to be a fun, carefree evening. Alma loves Romanoff's and always orders champagne, fine wine, and the most expensive things on the menu.

The next morning, Werfel wakes up full of confidence. The fighting in Europe is over, and the Werfels want to return home as soon as possible—perhaps for good. For the past few days, they've been pondering where they should go first. Vienna, London, and Rome are at the top of their wish list, and they're also considering a trip to Werfel's birthplace, Prague. After lunch, Werfel lies down. Alma is waiting for friends for coffee, and before they arrive, she checks on her husband, who has gotten up in the meantime and is working on a manuscript at his desk.

But when Alma returns to his study shortly after 6:00 p.m., he's lying lifeless on the floor. Efforts to revive him are in vain. Franz Werfel's heart has stopped beating.

"Sunday, August 26—we're both extremely lazy and let things go as they may," Annemarie von Duhn writes in her diary. "We have a lot to do, but we can't decide to do anything. There's no point." Annemarie and her husband Johann are very worried about the future. The Red Army still occupies Babelsberg, where they live, and Soviet soldiers have now commandeered the houses to the left and right of their own. This causes Johann in particular sleepless nights. When will it be their turn? Fearing the worst, Johann recently hastened to remove large, valuable sections of his library from his home, distributing them to acquaintances. But after getting the impression that the books weren't safe there either, he took them back and returned them to their original place. "All the back and forth is pointless," Annemarie complains, "especially when you consider that we probably won't be able to stay in Germany in the long term and will have to leave most of our things behind when we emigrate."[45]

V

Werfel's funeral takes place on the afternoon of August 29, three days after his death, with more than one hundred guests, including the Manns, conductor Otto Klemperer, and composers Arnold Schönberg and Igor Stravinsky. Bruno Walter and singer Lotte Lehmann have agreed to provide the music. But when Albrecht Joseph, Franz Werfel's secretary of many years, arrives to pick Alma up by car, she refuses to attend the ceremony. "I'm not going," she declares curtly. She sits emotionlessly at Werfel's desk, working. When Albrecht Joseph asks if he's heard correctly, she replies that she didn't attend Gustav Mahler's funeral or her daughter Manon's either. "I never go!"[46]

The funeral service turns into something of a farce. Almost the entire German-speaking exile community waits in the overcrowded chapel for the ceremony to begin, but nothing happens. Neither the grieving widow nor Father Georg Moenius, a friend of the Werfels who is supposed to conduct the ceremony, have appeared. An organist plays contemplative music and is eventually replaced by Walter, who performs a few short piano pieces by Franz Schubert, which were among Werfel's favorites. When he's finished, there is an awkward silence. Alma and Moenius are nowhere to be seen. Walter then plays the Schubert pieces again, but even after that there is no sign of Moenius. Behind the stage, someone finds some sheet music of the kind of trivial mood music often played at funerals. Walter takes one look at it and refuses to play. Meanwhile, the funeral directors are running back and forth, visibly nervous. Another funeral is scheduled afterward, and they need the chapel.

When Moenius turns up, over an hour late, in clerical garb but without the widow, the funeral service can finally begin. Word quickly gets round that he was delayed by Alma editing his eulogy. Ignoring how late he was becoming, she made changes, deleting entire passages and composing digressive additions. "His speech was an amazing performance," Albrecht Joseph will recall. "The Church," says Moenius, "recognizes three kinds of baptism: the baptism by water, the baptism in emergency, which can be performed by any believing Catholic when there is no time to call a priest, and finally the baptism by desire which means that someone who in his last moments on this earth earnestly desires to be received into the Church can become a Christian by the mere force of this desire although no visible or audible rites are performed."[47] Many of those present exchange questioning looks. Why a discussion of baptismal rites at a funeral service for Franz Werfel? Is it supposed to mean that Werfel did not depart this world as a Jew? Is the pious clergyman implying that he and Alma "emergency baptized" Werfel after he died? This outrageous suspicion continues to preoccupy Albrecht. A few days after the bizarre funeral, he confronts Moenius and asks him point-blank whether such a baptism was the reason for Alma's lengthy revision of the eulogy. "He avoided a direct confirmation," Albrecht will remember, "but did not deny my assumption that she had insisted on this point."[48]

There's good reason to think that Alma may have baptized her dead husband. In any case, the idea had the backing of the Franciscan Father Cyrill Fischer, a friend of the Werfels in California who died in May and had been obsessed with the idea of persuading Werfel to convert to Christianity. A request he once made of Alma was certainly clear enough. "Perhaps you should be the angel," Father Cyrill wrote in a 1943 letter, "who shows him the way to the Christ Child, and St. Bernadette will guide you and the Blessed Virgin, the Mother of the Savior of the World, will bless you a thousand times over." And to ensure that Alma knew what to do if the situation turned urgent—Werfel had already suffered a potentially fatal heart attack in September 1943—Father Cyril explained the necessary steps. "In an emergency, if his condition worsens unexpectedly, you can baptize him yourself with the words: 'Franz, I baptize you in the name of the Father and of the Son and of the Holy Spirit' and, while you say these words, sprinkle him lightly with consecrated water or even with plain water in the shape of a cross (not just sprinkle him!). I think it would not be an outrage, but rather a joy and reassurance for Franz and you yourself."[49]

Moenius is also part of the story. He too aspired to convert Jewish emigrants to the Catholic Church. "When

Werfel died he immediately came to us, the very next day, and wanted to convert Lion to Catholicism," Marta Feuchtwanger, the wife of German novelist Lion Feuchtwanger, will recall. "The king is dead, long live the king!"[50]

Thanks to the instructions given her by the two clergymen, Alma would have known how to baptize Werfel when she found him lying on the floor. But did she do it? Shortly after the funeral service, following a conversation with Alma, German scholar Adolf D. Klarmann, a longtime friend of Werfel's, jots down an explosive piece of news in his notebook: "F.W. was baptized after his death."[51] To be on the safe side, Klarmann writes, Alma made him promise to keep this secret to himself under all circumstances. He underlines the word "secret" twice in his notebook. He would keep his vow until the end of his days.

The mourners at Pierce Brothers Funeral Home have no idea of any of this. Thomas Mann, who appreciated Werfel and almost—but only almost—regarded him as a literary equal, notes in his diary: "Shaken nerves and cried."[52] Igor Stravinsky was also deeply moved. He had admired Werfel as a man with a keen musical mind, he would later recall, writing: "Werfel was an attractive person, with large, lucid, magnetic eyes—indeed, his eyes were the most beautiful I ever have seen, as his teeth were the most horrible." Stravinsky also remembered the funeral service as the event "that confronted me for the first time in thirty-three years with the angry, tortured, burning face of Arnold Schoenberg."[53]

V

According to the Berlin State Health Office, in August 1945, 23,471 cattle, 441 calves, 123 pigs, 33,832 sheep and 1 goat were slaughtered in the city.[54]

V

September 2 is unseasonably cool in Tokyo. When Toshikazu Kase leaves his house at around 5:00 a.m. and looks up at the sky, he sees nothing but gray clouds hanging so low that they seem close enough to touch. The gloomy weather suits the task that forty-two-year-old Kase has before him today. The diplomat is part of a delegation of eleven charged with burying the old Japanese empire. The group is led by Foreign Minister Mamoru Shigemitsu and Chief of the Army Staff Yoshijirō Umezu. Three representatives each from the Foreign Ministry, the army, and the navy make up the other nine delegates. In a few hours—at 9:00 a.m. sharp—the men will sign the Japanese declaration of surrender. The job at hand is particularly intolerable for the fanatic Umezu. When he learned of his task, Emperor Hirohito had to intervene personally to prevent him from committing *seppuku*.

President Truman has decided that the ceremony in Tokyo Bay should take place on board the American battleship *Missouri*. Missouri is the name of his home state, the president explains, and his daughter, Margaret, once christened the ship. Major events in world history sometimes have very personal details.

At 8:56 a.m., a barge with the Japanese delegation docks alongside the *Missouri*. The fifty-eight-year-old Shigemitsu, who lost his right leg in an assassination attempt in 1932 and has needed a prosthesis ever since, has great difficulty climbing the ladder to the *Missouri*'s main deck. Once there, the Japanese line up in three rows in front of a table covered in green cloth, on which the surrender document lies in duplicate. Mamoru Shigemitsu, Katsuo Okazaki from the Foreign Ministry, and Kase are wearing top hats, cutaways, and dark pants that make them look like figures from a time long gone by. "We waited a few minutes, standing in the public gaze like penitent boys awaiting the dreaded schoolmaster," Kase will later recall. "I tried to preserve the dignity of defeat but it was difficult and every minute seemed to contain ages."[55]

Douglas MacArthur appears. The sixty-five-year-old, highly decorated general served as commander-in-chief of the American forces in the Pacific and will soon play a decisive role in shaping the Japanese postwar order as Allied supreme commander. If MacArthur hadn't existed in reality, Hollywood would have invented him. He is not only the man of the hour, but also a dashing figure, whose trademarks include a field marshal's cap, gold-rimmed sunglasses like those worn by movie stars, and his signature corncob pipe. When he carries a riding crop, as he sometimes does, he looks like a colonial ruler. MacArthur is considered as assertive as he is vain. He loves making a grand entrance and

The end of the Second World War. A Japanese delegation led by Foreign Minister Mamoru Shigemitsu and Army Chief of Staff Yoshijirō Umezu arrives in Tokyo Bay aboard the USS Missouri *to sign the instrument of surrender.*

symbolically demonstrating his power. But he's also said to be decent and fair to his subordinates.

When asked a few minutes before the ceremony whether he and his officers will don ties, MacArthur snaps back that since the war was fought without ties, the surrender will take place without ties as well. He and his officers dress in khaki pants and long-sleeved open-necked shirts, while the enlisted men wear white trousers and sweaters.

Everything takes place very quickly. General MacArthur opens the proceedings, which start with the American national anthem. He then gives a short, powerful speech: "It is my earnest hope, and indeed the hope of all mankind, that from this solemn occasion a better world shall emerge out of the blood and carnage of the past, a world founded upon faith and understanding, a world dedicated to the dignity of man and the fulfillment of his most cherished wish for freedom, tolerance and justice."[56]

MacArthur instructs the Japanese to sign the surrender document on the table. Shigemitsu is initially unclear where exactly he should sign, so MacArthur's chief of staff, General Richard Sutherland, shows him the correct line. When all the representatives have added their signatures, MacArthur solemnly announces: "Let us pray that Peace be now restored to the world, and that God will preserve it always. These proceedings are closed."[57] The ceremony is over after less than ten minutes. With the Japanese surrender, the Second World War ends exactly six years to the day after it broke out. "At that moment the skies parted and the sun shone brightly through the layers of clouds," Kase will remember.[58] As the Japanese disembark and return to their vessel, a steady roar can be heard, growing closer and closer and intensifying into a din. As Kase looks up, he sees countless aircraft—including 450 carriers and 600 B-29 bombers—seeing off the Japanese delegation with an overwhelming display of American air power. Douglas MacArthur is nothing if not true to himself.

History is once again being made in Berlin. The scene is the Titania-Palast, a giant movie theater the Berlin Philharmonic has been using as a concert hall. When conductor Rudolph Dunbar steps in front of the orchestra on the morning of September 2, many concertgoers rub their eyes in amazement. It's not so much the fact that the forty-six-year-old appears in an American military uniform, but that he's African-American. Born in British Guiana, Dunbar studied the clarinet in New York before settling in Paris as a jazz musician. He then took lessons with the legendary conductor Felix Weingartner in Vienna. Dunbar has been based in London since 1931, where he works for the BBC and conducted a concert by the London Philharmonic Orchestra at the Royal Albert Hall in 1942. At some point, he attracted the notice of Leo Borchard, who invited him to perform with his Berlin Philharmonic in the early summer of 1945, causing *Time* magazine to snipe: "U.S. occupation authorities were all for it, though their interest was more in teaching the Germans a lesson in racial tolerance than in Dunbar's musicianship.[59] Borchard is now dead, but the Philharmonic honors the invitation. It may have helped that Dunbar declared in advance that he would bring a new contrabassoon that he'll donate to the orchestra—which lost many of its instruments in air raids.

It's shortly after 10:30 a.m. when Rudolph looks down into the orchestra pit and raises his baton. The concert begins with "The Star-Spangled Banner." The semi-weekly report of the American Information Control Division, which oversees cultural life in liberated Germany, will state afterward that most of the audience rose from their seats for the American national anthem, and that those who didn't had guilty looks on their faces, almost as if they were expecting the Gestapo to show up.[60]

Carl Maria von Weber's Oberon Overture follows, and it will conclude Tchaikovsky's Pathétique Symphony. The Philharmonic has played both these pieces countless times. However, even these veteran musicians break new ground with the work they play before the interval. It is William Grant Still's Afro-American Symphony, which in 1931 became the first composition by a Black American ever to be premiered by a major orchestra. The almost half-hour work blends blues and spirituals from Stills' homeland with symphonic elements. These previously unheard sounds were so well received by the audience that Rudolph is called out five times for a post-performance bow. The musicians are happy as well. "Now at last I understand your American jazz," remarks the orchestra's solo flautist.[61] But the orchestra never offers Rudolph a return engagement, although its new contrabassoon certainly sounds excellent.

V

Thomas Mann has been grumpy for days. If he's not being tormented by a severe nasal congestion, the late summer weather exhausts him. In any case, the septuagenarian is prone to getting upset. In such moments, he's so thin-skinned that even trifles can have negative consequences. "I also suffer mentally and physically," he once complained, "from the fact that size 4 in undergarments is too small for me, and size 5 too big."[62] He's also quick to blow his top if his dog doesn't do as he wants. "Quarrel with the poodle because of his disobedience after finding repulsive things," he confesses to his diary during the war. "Decided not to care anymore."[63]

While he's able to ignore his four-legged friend's unruliness, after the war he finds it difficult to deal with another vexed issue. At the beginning of August, the writer Walter von Molo sent Mann an open letter asking him to return to Germany. "Please, come soon," the appeal read. "Look upon the faces furrowed with grief, see the unspeakable suffering in the eyes of the many who did not take part in the glorification of our dark side, who weren't able to leave their native land because many millions of people here had no other place than at home, in what gradually became a large concentration camp, where there were soon only gradations of guards and inmates."[64]

Thomas Mann would prefer not to answer the letter at all, but that's impossible. Walter von Molo is no stranger. The two know each other from the literature division of the Prussian Academy of Arts, of which Molo served as deputy president. Now sixty-five years old, Molo has made a name for himself as the author of historical novels such as *Friedrich the Great at War, Schiller in Leipzig,* and *Luther, The Man*—works that sold fantastically in the Wilhelmine era and the Weimar Republic and were often mocked. "No one can ignore this novel," critic Kurt Tucholsky wrote acidly of one of Molo's efforts. "It just keeps coming back to haunt you."[65]

Molo was by no means a dyed-in-the-wool Nazi, although he was initially sympathetic to the regime. Soon after Hitler came to power, he withdrew into private life but remained a member of the Academy and continued to publish. He considered himself an "inner emigrant," i.e. someone who did not actively oppose or support the Third Reich. Thomas Mann has little time for this idea.

It takes the Nobel Prize winner several weeks to pen his reply to Molo. "Worked on the letter to Germany mornings and afternoons," he writes in his diary at the beginning of September.[66] He was obviously finding it difficult. "Experimenting with the letter to Germany, half of which misses the mark."[67] He rejects and discards a first version of the missive. Only then does he come up with a reply he deems fit to be printed.

He should be pleased that Germany wants him back, Mann begins politely, before immediately asking: "Can these twelve years and what resulted from them be wiped off the slate, and can we pretend they didn't happen?" Though his language occasionally sounds conciliatory, he attacks the representatives of "inner emigration" head-on: "All of you who swore allegiance to the 'charismatic leader' (appalling, appalling, besotted presumption!) and practiced culture under Goebbels did not go through the cardiac asthma of exile, the uprooting, the nervous terrors of homelessness. I'm not forgetting that you later went through much worse, which I escaped, but you didn't know that." Mann finds it distasteful of contemporaries like Molo to believe it was possible to be artistically active under Hitler's rule and remain upstanding. "It may be a bias, but in my eyes, those books that could be printed at all in Germany from 1933 to 1945 are beyond worthless and should never be picked up," he writes. "There is a smell of blood and shame about them. They should all be disposed of."

The last sentence must have particularly hurt von Molo. Although Mann's letter is ostensibly addressed specifically to his colleague, it's really aimed at all Germans, to whom he is now issuing an unmistakable rebuff. "Today I am an American citizen, and long before Germany's terrible defeat, I declared publicly and privately that I had no intention of ever turning my back on America again."[68] That leaves nothing to be desired in terms of clarity. Mann also expressed his thoughts on Molo and the other cultural figures who remained in Germany after 1933 in a letter to the stage designer Emil Preetorius. There he wrote: "They all took part, they all profited, they all believed in the permanence of the abominable, which they never really perceived as abominable and detested. And now they are playing the heroes and martyrs who stayed with Germany and suffered with it, while we have made ourselves comfortable in loges of foreign countries, etc., etc. What massive impertinence."[69]

V

Franz Werfel would have turned fifty-five years old on September 10. Her late husband's birthday is understandably a painful occasion for Alma Mahler-Werfel. "How can it be that I should no longer hear that voice, that I should no longer look into those eyes that have shone in my eyes for twenty-seven years," she laments to her friend Friedrich Torberg in New York.[70] Werfel's death brings dramatic change to Alma's life. Until then, all her love and care had gone toward her long-ailing husband, but now she's alone in a foreign country with a language still foreign to her. She would never think to profess to being an American citizen, as Thomas Mann did. And what will become of the large circle of friends, lavish dinner parties, and frequent visits to Romanoff's, when the actual center of all the social commotion is no longer? "As always, it's dull as puke here," she complains to Torberg, "if you didn't have inner strength to draw on, you'd string yourself up!"[71]

She would love to return to Vienna, but for the time being travel to Europe is reserved for military personnel. Alma is so desperate with loneliness in her villa in Beverly Hills that she flees to New York. Manhattan at least reminds her of the Old World. Here distances are short, many things can be done on foot, and the Metropolitan Opera and the Philharmonic are only a few minutes away by cab. Initially she stays at the chic Hotel St. Moritz before moving to the residential hotel The Alrae on 64th Street between Madison and Park Avenue, where she plans to spend the next few months.

Along with old acquaintances like Erich Maria Remarque, Marlene Dietrich, Alfred Polgar, and Carl Zuckmayer, she sees Torberg and his new girlfriend, Marietta Bellak, almost every day. Alma is keen to get to know the twenty-four-year-old Marietta, whom Torberg, twelve years her senior, had previously described as follows: "She is young, blonde, known for being pretty, nature- and animal-loving, funny, lively, noisy, eager, knowledgeable, thoughtful, and the opposite of those qualities, but above all—because being once bitten, twice shy, and fearful of American women—she is from Vienna. Her parents, as is sometimes the case in good Jewish homes in exile, live in discord." Marietta was also "extremely well-mannered," Torberg wrote, adding: "Fluent French in all rooms. Wants to go back, but doesn't know where. Nor do I. Hence the common interests."[72]

Marietta also looks forward to her first encounter with the famous Mrs. Mahler-Werfel with excitement. She has heard and read a lot about Alma's love life: That she was married to composer Gustav Mahler, architect Walter Gropius, and writer Franz Werfel and had an *amour fou* with the painter Oskar Kokoschka. The number of Alma's affairs is legion, "not including those that got swept away by the river," Torberg once laughingly explains to his girlfriend, quoting a line from Friedrich Schiller's *Maid of Orleans*.

When the two women meet for the first time in New York, Alma, as she often did, revealed her generous side. "We each got a lobster," Marietta will recall of the dinner. "I ate mine, while she just broke hers up because she never ate anything, just drank. She drank a lot of champagne, then a lot of Benedictine, and I sat on the floor at her feet after dinner and she cuddled my head and said: 'my little pet.' She always said that to people she liked. 'My little pet, you're not really Jewish, are you?' I said: 'Yes, Alma, I am. On both sides—father and mother.' She really was a complete anti-Semite. If she liked someone, she didn't want to admit that. And she was drunk too. She tried to force me to tell her that I was born Roman Catholic. I couldn't give her the pleasure."[73]

How is Rudi Bach doing? Stephen Spender lost sight of the seriously ill boy when he traveled to Paris in August to establish contacts between British and French intellectuals. Now—at the end of September—Stephen is back in Bonn and remembers the little patient. At the hospital, Stephen is told that Rudi has made a full recovery and is back living with his parents in a village between Cologne and Bonn. Stephen gets the Bachs' address and plans to pay the family a visit as soon as possible.

When he rings the doorbell, Mrs. Bach opens the door and is delighted to see him again. "Mr. Spender is here," she calls out, folding her hands as if in prayer. Showering him with praise for saving her Rudi's life, she pulls Stephen over the threshold and leads him into the living room, where the family is sitting at a large round table over coffee and cake. Stephen has often noticed that there is an abundance of food in the countryside, while supplies in the cities are often precarious. But the amount of fresh fruit cake, which seems to take up a good half of the table, leaves him temporarily speechless.

Stephen lets his eyes wander around the room. Where is Rudi? The chubby boy sitting at the table, eating one piece of cake after another, has nothing in common with the emaciated and dying boy in the hospital, yet—it's Rudi! Stephen is shocked. As happy as he is that Rudi has recovered, he finds the boy's obesity repulsive.

"He was really incredibly fat, with bulging cheeks, bulging thighs, and a complexion like a suet pudding," Stephen will later recall. Stephen is embarrassed and makes a few rather awkward remarks about Rudi's appetite.[74] "Oh, this is nothing," Rudi replies confidently. "I shall soon be much fatter. I am not properly well yet; only convalescent."[75] His heart is weak, he precociously informs his visitor, so he has to rest, avoid exertion himself and, above all, eat a lot.

While Rudi balances another piece of cake on his fork, Mrs. Bach begins to lament the supposed depravity of her time. She rejects all kinds of superficial entertainment, she says, her voice suddenly turning harsh. She was recently in Bonn and saw posters advertising a colorful evening of cabaret. Imagine that, Ms. Bach grumbles, cabaret of all things! She pronounces "cabaret" as if it were a dirty word one shouldn't even think. When Stephen counters that it's nice people are having fun again, she waves him off. "The least one would expect, after all that the Germans have done, is that they should be compelled to have good music, good books, good theatre; nothing but what is good," she says severely. "Mozart, Beethoven, Goethe. Nothing else should be allowed."[76]

Stephen is about to tell his hostess that cultural censorship cannot be the answer to crimes of National Socialism, but he's heard enough. The sight of obese Rudi and his mother's grotesque talk bother him so much that he regrets having come at all. On the drive back to Bonn, Mrs. Bach's words about composers like Mozart and poets like Goethe echo in him. And in his mind's eye he sees a little boy who, thanks to his help, has escaped death and now devours his sixth piece of fruitcake. Or is it already the eighth?

V

Trouble is brewing in Cologne. For weeks Konrad Adenauer has been at odds with the British military administration,

Konrad Adenauer discusses the reconstruction of Cologne at a drawing board. The sixty-nine-year-old has recently been re-elected Lord Mayor of the city, a position he held previously before 1933. "The imagination has to be provided for."

which is demanding that the Cologne mayor cut down the trees in the parks and ring roads and make the wood available to the population as fuel. Adenauer strictly rejects the idea. It was he after all, who had this ring of greenery, over twenty kilometers long and about one kilometer wide, planted around the city during his first term as mayor in the 1920s. This area is very important for the health of the population. "The amount of wood that would have been provided by cutting down the trees would have been a drop in the bucket in my opinion, given the coal shortage in Cologne," he will remember countering. "The fuel shortage would by no means have been even remotely solved."[77] Adenauer demands, instead, that confiscated coal stocks be released.

He's playing with fire. What Adenauer doesn't know is that the British have been looking for a pretext to get rid of him for some time now. The reason is less his work for the city than his contacts with the American and French military administrations, which are a thorn in their side. The Americans, who had been in charge in Cologne until June 21, had a close relationship with Adenauer, and the sixty-nine-year-old continues to be on cordial terms with them. At the end of August, he met the former American military governor of Cologne, John K. Patterson, for an exchange of ideas. This was part of a dual strategy. A few days later, on September 2, he had a memorandum on economic, cultural, and political cooperation with France presented via an intermediary to French General Pierre Billotte. The paper revived ideas that he had already developed during the Weimar Republic.

Close economic and cultural ties between the two countries should address French needs for security while undermining excessive French demands for reparations and support for Rhenish separatist movements in Germany. Over the course of September, Adenauer's contacts with French occupation authorities have become ever closer. He meets several times with French military chaplain Lucien Joseph Stenger, an envoy of French military headquarters. There are even rumors of a top-secret meeting with Charles de Gaulle at Maria Laach Abbey, although there's probably nothing to them. Meanwhile, the English are realizing that Adenauer's political ambitions are no longer limited to the city level.

Around this time, another memorandum warning against Adenauer by retired General Sir Charles Fergusson circulates at British headquarters. Fergusson, now eighty years old, served the British military governor in Cologne for seven months after the end of the First World War and had disliked Adenauer ever since. "His demeanour was stiff (as was ours) and correct—but he made no pretence of anything but hatred of the British," Ferguson will remember from that time. Although Adenauer was "a man of great influence and undeniable ability," he should not be trusted under any circumstances, Ferguson proposes. "He is clever, cunning, a born intriguer, and dangerous. I suggest that too much reliance should not be placed on him, and that in their dealing with him our authorities should be on their guard."[78]

The memorandum lands on Gerald Templer's desk in Lübbecke in the western German region of Westphalia. As the forty-seven-year-old general with the prominent cheekbones and wideset eyes reads Fergusson's reckoning with Adenauer, he strokes a dachshund sitting on his lap in short, steady pats. When Templer visits Cologne a few days later, he's horrified. The cathedral city is in dire shape and holds the sad record for the least amount of rubble removed from an urban area. Templer is the de facto head of government in the British occupation zone, and Fergusson's memorandum has arrived just at the right time. Templer orders Brigadier General John Barraclough, the military governor of the Province of North Rhine, to get rid of Adenauer as quickly as possible. At the moment, he's more inclined to dismiss Adenauer because of "incompetence" than because of political undesirability, Barraclough writes to headquarters.[79]

The brigadier general has Adenauer's official severance papers drawn up. "In my opinion you have failed in your duty to the people of Cologne," the document reads. "You are therefore dismissed today from your appointment as Oberbürgermeister [Lord Mayor] of Cologne."[80] Adenauer is also ordered to leave the city and banned from all political activity. In the event of noncompliance, he will be tried before a military court. Barraclough personally presents and reads out the document to Adenauer on October 6. During the degrading ceremony, in which Adenauer is forbidden to sit down, he shows no emotion whatsoever and stands directly in front of Barraclough with his hands folded. When he is done reading, the brigadier general finally asks if Adenauer has anything to say. Adenauer's reply: "No!"

V

The number of suicides in Berlin continues to fall. While 3,881 men and women committed suicide in April, the figure was 977 in May, 367 in June, 340 in July, and 263 in August. In September, 196 people voluntarily ended their lives.[81]

V

Michael Thomas has to pause to catch his breath after climbing the fifty-nine steps from Zenningsweg to the white villa in Rhöndorf on the Rhine. He is not alone. Old or young, fat or thin, sick or healthy—everyone who wishes to speak to the master of the house has to take on this ascent. Some visitors submit to these fifty-nine steps silently, while others make mocking remarks about "Rhenish Obersalzberg"—a cutting comparison to Hitler's Alpine getaway. Michael briefly adjusts his uniform, then rings the bell.[82] After a short time, a man in a priest's cassock opens the door. "I'm from military government headquarters and would like to speak to your father," says the visitor.[83] The priest nods and leads him into a small room with light-colored Biedermeier furniture. There Konrad Adenauer is sitting in an armchair.

Michael introduces himself. Perhaps he tells him that he's from Berlin and that his real name is Ulrich Hollaender, that his father, Felix, was a famous writer and theater director in the Weimar Republic, that cultural greats such as the director Max Reinhardt, the actors Emil Jannings, Fritzi

Massary, and Käthe Dorsch frequented his boyhood home, and that the writer Gerhart Hauptmann was a close friend of the family. Michael might tell Adenauer how, more or less by chance, he was stranded in England three days before the outbreak of the Second World War, how he joined the British military, changed his name out of concern for his mother, who lives in Berlin, and then simply kept it. Ulrich Hollaender became Michael Thomas, but none of that is important now. Michael didn't climb all those stairs to talk about himself. He has set his mind on getting to know Konrad Adenauer, whom he heard so much about in his school and university days.

The master of the house is still very stunned by his harsh dismissal at the hands of Barraclough. "Our paratroopers aren't known for their intelligence either, even if they're generals," Adenauer complains in his singsong Rhenish accent. "But that can't be the whole explanation. It cannot be that such a brigadier general can fire a man like me. This has to be a directive from the Foreign Office. Perhaps they think I've been secretly meeting with de Gaulle. But I didn't meet with de Gaulle!"

Adenauer obviously feels guilty about his contacts with the French and wants to test his visitor, but Michael doesn't respond. He has been a great friend to the English, Adenauer continues. During the Third Reich, he even hid a silk English flag in his garden. He's saved it for posterity. And what thanks has he gotten? The English used to be "gentlemen," but that was a long time ago.

When Michael asked what he planned to do in the future, Adenauer replies: "As you can see, I'm an old man, I don't have any political ambitions anymore." Michael shoots back: "Mr. Adenauer, I'm not buying it!"[84] A quickly suppressed smile flits across Adenauer's long, lean face.

A summer of freedom comes to an end. It's an important period in the history of the world, but it was utterly unremarkable in terms of the weather. In Berlin in June, July, and August 1945, there were a total of thirty-one summer days above twenty-five degrees Celsius and seven above thirty degrees Celsius. This is neither particularly hot nor cold. In this respect you could also say it was a summer like any other.

NOTES

At the Abyss

1. Margaret Truman, *Harry S. Truman* (Morrow, 1973), 241.

2. Harry S. Truman, *Memoirs. Volume 1, The Year of Decisions* (Doubleday, 1955), 124n.

3. Frank S. Adams, "Germany Surrenders. New Yorkers Massed Under Symbol of Liberty," *The New York Times*, May 8, 1945, p. 1.

4. Alfred Döblin, *Ausgewählte Werke. Vol. 13, Briefe* (Walter Verlag, 1970), 315n.

5. Deutsches Tagebucharchiv Emmendingen, DTA 1457–1, p. 20.

6. Ibid., 36.

7. Ibid., 25.

8. Ibid., 37n.

9. Robert Rhodes James, ed., *Winston S. Churchill. His complete speeches*, vol. 7 (Chelsea House Publishers, 1974), 7153.

10. Ibid., 7155.

11. Charles de Gaulle, *Discours et Messages. Pendant la guerre, Juin 1940–Janvier 1946* (Plon, 1970), 545n.

12. War Cabinet, 59th Conclusions, 7. May 1945, The National Archives, CAB 65/50/22.

13. Winston Churchill to Clement Attlee and Anthony Eden, May 21, 1943, Churchill Archives Centre, CHAR 20/128/27–28.

14. Alexander Fischer, ed., *Teheran, Jalta, Potsdam. Die sowjetischen Protokolle von den Kriegskonferenzen der "Großen Drei"* (Wissenschaft, 1968), 114.

15. Martin Gilbert, *The Day the War Ended. VE-Day 1945 in Europe and Around the World* (Henry Holt & Co., 1995), 220.

16. Foreign Office telegram to Paris, No 916, The National Archives, FO 954/9B/553.

17. Hauptamt für Statistik Gross-Berlin, ed., *Zahlen zeigen Zeitgeschehen. Berlin 1945–1947* (Hauptamt für Statistik Gross-Berlin, 1947), 47.

18. Curt Riess, *Das war ein Leben!* Erinnerungen (Albert Langen, 1986), 327.

19. Klaus Mann, *Der Wendepunkt. Ein Lebensbericht* (Rowohlt, 2014), 657. [Published in English as *The Turning Point: Thirty-five Years in This Century* (L. B. Fischer, 1942).]

20. Ibid., 658.

21. Ibid., 242

22. Thomas Mann, *Tagebücher. 1937–1939*, ed. Peter de Mendelssohn (S. Fischer, 1980), 242.

23. Thomas Mann, *Tagebücher. 1944–1.4.1946*, ed. Inge Jens (S. Fischer, 1986), 202.

24. Ibid.

25. Erich Kästner, *Notabene 45. Ein Tagebuch* (Atrium, 2017), 147.

26. Ibid., 147n.

27. Ibid., 147.

28. Margot Friedländer, *"Versuche dein Leben zu machen." Als Jüdin versteckt in Berlin* (Rowohlt Taschenbuch, 2008), 218.

29. Georgi K. Zhukow, *Reminiscences and Reflections*, vol. 2 (Progress Publishers, 1985), 400.

30. *Neue Zürcher Zeitung*, May, 10 1945.

31. Konstantin Simonow, *Kriegstagebücher 1942–1945* (Kindler Verlag, 1982), 810.

32. Walter Görlitz, ed., *Generalfeldmarschall Keitel—Verbrecher oder Offizier? Erinnerungen, Briefe, Dokumente des Chefs OKW* (Musterschmidt Verlag, 1961), 378.

33. Josef Stalin, *Reden, Interviews, Telegramme, Befehle, Briefe und Botschaften. Mai 1945–Oktober 1952* (Parteihochschule Karl Marx, 1952), p. 3n.

34. Swetlana Allilujewa, *Zwanzig Briefe an einen Freund* (Verlag Fritz Molden, 1967), 257.

35. Ibid., 258.

36. Alfred Misselhorn, *Kriegsende und Gefangenschaft*, in LeMO-Zeitzeugen, Lebendiges Museum Online, Stiftung Haus der Geschichte der Bundesrepublik Deutschland.

37. Elke Scherstjanoi, ed., *Rotarmisten schreiben aus Deutschland. Briefe von der Front (1945) und historische Analysen* (De Gruyter Saur, 2004), 172n.

38. Mann, *Der Wendepunkt*, 668n.

39. Ibid., 669n.

40. Michael Assmann, ed., *Thomas Mann, Erich von Kahler. Briefwechsel 1931–1955* (Luchterhand Literaturverlag, 1993), 80.

41. Ruth Andreas-Friedrich, *Schauplatz Berlin. Tagebuchaufzeichnungen 1945–1948* (Suhrkamp, 1986), 29.

42. Lys Symonette and Kim H. Kowalke, eds., *Speak Low When You Speak Love: The Letters of Kurt Weill and Lotte Lenya* (University of California Press, 1996), 458.

43. Ibid., 427.

44. Ibid., 443

45. Mann, *Tagebücher. 1944–1.4.1946*, 204.

46. Scherstjanoi, *Rotarmisten schreiben aus Deutschland*, 179n.

47. Mann, *Der Wendepunkt*, 670.

48. Ibid, 671.

49. Ibid., 671n.

50. Ibid., 672.

51. Ibid., 670.

52. Ibid., 671n.

53. Ibid., 673.

54. Ibid., 673.

55. Ibid., 674.

56. Marion Beyer, Jürgen May, and Walter Werbeck, eds., *Richard Strauss. Späte Aufzeichnungen* (Schott Music, 2016), 310.

57. "Glenn Gould Stories: Angels, Iconoclasts, and Alter Egos," August 28, 2022. The Glenn Gould Foundation (www.glenngould.ca). Accessed November 16, 2025.

58. Mann, *Der Wendepunkt*, 682.

59. Andreas-Friedrich, *Schauplatz Berlin*, 34.

60. Ibid., 36n.

61. Scherstjanoi, *Rotarmisten schreiben aus Deutschland*, 182.

62. Deutsches Tagebucharchiv Emmendingen, DTA 1457–1, p. 60.

63. Winston G. Ramsey, "Himmler's Suicide," *After the Battle*, Nr. 14, 15. August 1976, p. 32.

64. Ibid., 34.

65. Ibid., 35.

66. Paul van Stemann, "Himmler's Night of Reckoning," *Independent*, May 20, 1995.

67. Ramsey, "Himmler's Suicide," 35.

68. Andreas-Friedrich, *Schauplatz Berlin*, 38.

69. Ibid., p. 30.

70. Peter Muck, *Einhundert Jahre Berliner Philharmonisches Orchester. Darstellung in Dokumenten*, vol. 2 (H. Schneider 1982), 189.

71. Andreas-Friedrich, *Schauplatz Berlin*, p. 42.

72. Deutsches Tagebucharchiv Emmendingen, DTA 1457–1, S. 68.

73. *Foreign Relations of the United States. Diplomatic Papers, The Conference of Berlin 1945*, vol. 1 (United States Government Printing Office 1960), 8n.

74. Ibid., p. 87.

75. *Berliner Zeitung*, May 27, 1945, p. 4.

76. Deutsches Tagebucharchiv Emmendingen, DTA 1457–1, p. 72n.

77. Ibid., p. 73.

78. Hauptamt für Statistik Gross-Berlin, *Zahlen zeigen Zeitgeschehen*, 39.

Friends and Enemies

1. Willi Schaeffers, *Tingeltangel. Ein Leben für die Kleinkunst* (Broschek, 1959), 198.

2. Brewster S. Chamberlin, *Kultur auf Trümmern. Berliner Berichte der amerikanischen Information Control Section Juli–Dezember 1945* (Deutsche Verlags-Anstalt, 1979), 36.

3. Brigitte Mira, *Kleine Frau—was nun? Erinnerungen an ein buntes Leben* (Ullsetin Verlag, 1988), 93.

4. Hans Jürgen Syberberg, *Winifred Wagner and the History of the Wahnfried House 1914–1975*, video.

5. Mann, *Der Wendepunkt*, 683n.

6. Deutsches Tagebucharchiv Emmendingen, DTA 1457–1, p. 75.

7. Alexander Werth, *Russia at War 1941–1945* (Skyhorse, 1964), 983.

8. *Amtsblatt des Kontrollrats in Deutschland, Ergänzungsblatt Nr. 1* (Eigenverlag 1946), 7–9.

9. Lucius D. Clay, *Decision in Germany* (Doubleday, 1950), 23.

10. Werth, *Russia at War 1941–1945*, 986.

11. Hans Rudolf Vaget, *Thomas Mann, der Amerikaner* (S. Fischer, 2012), 241.

12. Ibid. p. 243.

13. Hans Rudolf Vaget, ed., *Thomas Mann, Agnes E. Meyer. Briefwechsel 1937–1955* (S. Fischer, 1992), 521.

14. Mann, *Tagebücher. 1944–1.4.1946*, 212.

15. Gottfried Bermann Fischer, *Bedroht—bewahrt. Der Weg eines Verlegers* (Fischer, 1982), 212.

16. Mann, *Tagebücher. 1944–1.4.1946*, 223.

17. Deutsches Tagebucharchiv Emmendingen, DTA 1457–1, p. 84.

18. Scherstjanoi, ed., *Rotarmisten schreiben aus Deutschland*, 187.

19. Misselhorn, Kriegsende und Gefangenschaft.

20. Investigation file, Landesarchiv Berlin, A Pr. Br. Rep. 030-03 No. 1558.

21. Kaspar Hauser [i.e. Kurt Tucholsky],"Die lieben Kinder," *Die Weltbühne*, February 19, 1929, p. 304.

22. John Julius Norwich, ed., *The Duff Cooper Diaries, 1915–1951* (Phoenix, 2005), 374.

23. Ibid., 292.

24. "My French": Diana Cooper, *Trumpets from the Steep* (Rupert Hart-Davis, 1960), 190.

25. *Stalin's Correspondence with Churchill, Attlee, Roosevelt and Truman 1941–45* (E. P. Dutton & Co., Inc., 1958), 364.

26. Hans von Lehndorff, *Ostpreußisches Tagebuch. Aufzeichnungen eines Arztes aus den Jahren 1945–1947* (dtv, 1967), 113.

27. Ibid., 145.

28. Ibid., 145.

29. Ibid., 106n.

30. Ermittlungsakte, Landesarchiv Berlin, A Pr. Br. Rep. 030-03 Nr. 1505.

31. Ermittlungsakte, Landesarchiv Berlin, A Pr. Br. Rep. 030-03 Nr. 1545.

32. Scherstjanoi, *Rotarmisten schreiben aus Deutschland*, 190.

33. Friedrich Torberg, *Liebste Freundin und Alma. Briefwechsel mit Alma Mahler-Werfel* (Ullstein, 1987), 214.

34. Mann, *Tagebücher. 1940–1943*, 412.

35. Peter Stephan Jungk, *Franz Werfel. Eine Lebensgeschichte* (S. Fischer, 1987), 301.

36. Ibid., 301.

37. Albrecht Joseph, "Werfel, Alma, Kokoschka, the actor George," William-Melnitz-Collection, University of California in Los Angeles, Charles E. Young Research Library, p. 24.

38. Ibid., p. 35.

39. Thomas Ehrsam and Regula Wyss, eds., *Thea Sternheim. Tagebücher 1903–1971*, with complete text CD-ROM (Wallsetin Verlag, 2002), CD-ROM version.

40. De Gaulle, *Discours et Messages. Pendant la guerre, Juin 1940–Janvier 1946*, 4.

41. Norwich, *The Duff Cooper Diaries, 1915–1951*, 375.

42. Ehrsam and Wyss, *Thea Sternheim. Tagebücher 1903–1971*, CD-ROM version.

43. *Billy Wilder. Eine Nahaufnahme* (Hoffman und Campe, 2006), 304. Translator's note: There are no English-language accounts of this encounter, so the passage has been translated from the German.

44. Ibid., 305.

45. Ibid., 305.

46. Ibid., 306.

47. Hanuš Burger, *Der Frühling war es wert. Erinnerungen* (Ullstein, 1977), 259.

48. Ibid, 257.

49. Ehrsam and Wyss, *Thea Sternheim. Tagebücher 1903–1971*, Vol. 3, 431.

50. Ibid., 431.

51. Ibid., 432.

52. Ibid., 432.

53. Katja Iken, Uwe Klußmann, and Eva-Maria Schnurr, eds., *Als Deutschland sich neu erfand. Die Nachkriegszeit 1945–1949* (Penguin 2019), 46.

54. Ibid., 50.

55. Ibid., 50.

56. Anonymous [Marta Hillers], *Eine Frau in Berlin. Tagebuch-Aufzeichnungen vom 20. April bis 22. Juni 1945* (btb 2008), 273.

57. Ibid., 274.

58. Ibid., 276.

59. Ibid., 174.

60. Ibid., 174.

61. Karl Deutmann, *Berlin 1945*, in LeMO-Zeitzeugen, Lebendiges Museum Online, Stiftung Haus der Geschichte der Bundesrepublik Deutschland.

62. Ibid.

63. Zhukov, *Reminiscences and Reflections*, vol. 2, 425.

64. Simon Sebag Montefiore, *Stalin. Am Hof des roten Zaren* (S. Fischer, 2005), 563.

65. Ibid., 565.

66. Misselhorn, *Kriegsende und Gefangenschaft*.

67. Ehrsam and Wyss, Thea Sternheim. *Tagebücher 1903–1971*, vol. 3, 433.

68. Ibid., 433.

69. Ibid., 433.

70. Klaus-Dietmar Henke, *Die amerikanische Besetzung Deutschlands* (De Gruyter Oldenbourg, 1996), 195n.

71. Ibid., 187.

72. Saul K. Padover, *Experiment in Germany* (Duell, Sloan & Pearce, 1946), 263.

73. Henke, *Die amerikanische Besetzung Deutschlands*, 204.

74. Friedländer, *Versuche dein Leben zu machen*, 224.

75. Ibid., 226.

76. Ibid., 227.

77. Ibid., 230n.

78. William L. Shirer, *The End of a Berlin Diary* (Popular Library, 1961), 39.

79. Ibid., 7.

80. Misselhorn, *Kriegsende und Gefangenschaft.*

Winners and Losers

1. Ermittlungsakte, Landesarchiv Berlin, A Pr. Br. Rep. 030-03 Nr. 1488.

2. Ibid.

3. Ibid.

4. Lord Moran, *Winston Churchill: Struggle for Survival 1945–1960* (Constable, 1966), 273.

5. Robert Rhodes James, ed., *Winston S. Churchill. His complete speeches*, vol. 7 (Chelsea House Publishers, 1974), 7172.

6. Moran, *Churchill*, 271.

7. Ibid., 271.

8. John Colville, *The Fringes of Power. Downing Street Diaries 1939–1955* (Hodder and Stoughton, 1985), 610.

9. Churchill, *Triumph and Tragedy* (Houghton Mifflin Company, 1953), 613.

10. Ermittlungsakte, Landesarchiv Berlin, A Pr. Br. Rep. 030-03 No. 1558.

11. Misselhorn, *Kriegsende und Gefangenschaft.*

12. Friedländer, *"Versuche dein Leben zu machen,"* 234.

13. George S. Patton, *Diaries, 1910–1945, Annotated transcripts 1943–1945*, 15 September 1945, George S. Patton Papers, Library of Congress.

14. Friedländer, *"Versuche dein Leben zu machen,"* 239.

15. Ibid., 237.

16. Heinz M. Zellermayer, *Alles zu meiner Zeit. Tagebuch-Erinnerungen an ein reiches Leben zwischen Gastlichkeit, Politik und Kunst* (Arne, 1990), 88.

17. "Wiederingangsetzung von Gaststätten und Betriebsküchen," 15. July 1945, Landesarchiv Berlin, F Rep. 280: 2790.

18. Zellermayer, *Alles zu meiner Zeit*, 148.

19. Ilse Zellermayer, *Drei Tenöre und ein Sopran. Mein Leben für die Oper* (Henschel, 2000), 202.

20. "Zellermayer, *Alles zu meiner Zeit*, 188.

21. Ibid., 149.

22. Misselhorn, *Kriegsende und Gefangenschaft.*

23. Eduard Mark, "'Today Has Been A Historical One.' Harry S. Truman's Diary of the Potsdam Conference," *Diplomatic History*, Vol. 4, Issue 3 (July 1980): 320. Truman initially referred to the building as the "Berlin White House." The Truman Library refers to it as the "Little White House."

24. Moran, *Churchill*, 287.

25. David Dilks, ed., *The Diaries of Sir Alexander Cadogan 1938–1945* (Cassell, 1971), 761.

26. Dimitri Wolkogonow, *Stalin, Triumph und Tragödie. Ein politisches Porträt* (Claassen, 1989), 672.

27. Mark, "'Today Has Been A Historical One,'" 320.

28. Ibid., 320.

29. Lansing Lamont, *Day of Trinity* (Atheneum, 1965), 226.

30. "Memorandum for Secretary of War," Leslie R. Groves to Henry Stimson, July 18, 1945, p. 5n, Harry S. Truman Library & Museum.

31. J. Robert Oppenheimer in Fred Freed, dir. *The Decision to Drop the Bomb*, NBC News, 1965, documentary.

32. Kenneth T. Bainbridge, "'All in our Time.' A foul and awesome display," *Bulletin of the Atomic Scientists*, May 1975, 46.

33. Mark, "'Today Has Been A Historical One,'" 321.

34. Ibid., 321.

35. Moran, *Churchill*, 290.

36. Ibid., 291.

37. Ibid., 298.

38. Oral History Interview with R. Gordon Arneson, Washington, D. C., 21 June 1989, Harry S. Truman Library & Museum.

39. *Potsdam Conference*, Vol. 2, 1360.

40. Deutsches Tagebucharchiv Emmendingen, DTA 2211–1, p. 21.

41. Truman, *Memoirs*, 267.

42. Mark, "'Today Has Been A Historical One,'" 322.

43. William D. Leahy, *I was there. The personal story of the chief of staff to Presidents Roosevelt and Truman based on his notes and diaries made at the time* (Whittlesey House, 1950), 465.

44. Mark, "'Today Has Been A Historical One,'" 323.

45. Churchill, *The Second World War*, 639.

46. Ibid., 639.

47. Mark, "'Today Has Been A Historical One,'" 322.

48. Beyer, May, and Webeck, eds., *Richard Strauss. Späte Aufzeichnungen*, 346.

49. Robert H. Ferrell, ed., *Dear Bess. The letters from Harry to Bess Truman 1910–1959* (W. W. Norton & Company, 1983), 520.

50. Dilks, *The Diaries of Sir Alexander Cadogan*, 767.

51. Andrei Gromyko, *Memoirs* (Doubleday, 1989), 113.

52. Deutsches Tagebucharchiv Emmendingen, DTA 2211–1, S. 21.

53. Monte M. Poen, ed., *Letters Home by Harry Truman* (G. P. Putnam's Sons, 1984), 193.

54. Leahy, *I was there*, 480n.

55. Ibid., 481.

56. Stephen Spender, *European Witness* (Hamish Hamilton Ltd., 1946), 21.

57. Robert Beachy, *Gay Berlin: Birthplace of a modern identity* (Vintage, 2015), 187.

58. Spender, *European Witness*, 49.

59. Ibid., 50.

60. Ibid., 50.

61. Ibid., 51.

62. Ibid., 53.

63. Moran, *Churchill*, 303.

64. Poen, *Letters Home by Harry Truman*, 194.

65. Mann, *Tagebücher. 1944–1.4.1946*, 234.

66. Truman, *Memoirs*, 346.

67. Churchill, *Triumph and Tragedy*, 670.

68. Deutsches Tagebucharchiv Emmendingen, DTA 1457–1, p. 113.

69. Dilks, *The Diaries of Sir Alexander Cadogan*, 772.

70. Churchill, *Triumph and Tragedy*, 674.

71. Ibid., 675.

72. Poen, *Letters Home by Harry Truman*, 195.

73. Chamberlin, *Kultur auf Trümmern*, 102.

74. Spender, *European Witness*, 76.

75. Hauptamt für Statistik Gross-Berlin, *Zahlen zeigen Zeitgeschehen*, 99.

76. Brett-Smith, *Berlin '45: The Grey City* (Macmillan, 1966), 115n.

77. Ferrell, ed., *Dear Bess*, 522n.

78. Hauptamt für Statistik Gross-Berlin, *Zahlen zeigen Zeitgeschehen*, 31.

The Bomb

1. Hugh Sidey, ed., *Prelude to Leadership. The European Diary of John F. Kennedy Summer 1945* (Regnery Pub, 1995), 43.

2. Oliver Lubrich, ed., *John F. Kennedy's Hidden Diary, Europe 1937: The Travel Journals of JFK and Kirk Lemoyne Billings* (Berghahn Books, 2023), 51.

3. Ibid., 49.

4. Ibid., 66.

5. Ibid., 58.

6. Sidley, *Prelude to Leadership*, 73.

7. Ibid., 73.

8. Ibid., 74.

9. Deutsches Tagebucharchiv Emmendingen, DTA 2211–1, p. 23.

10. Mann, *Tagebücher. 1944–1.4.1946*, 236.

11. George F. Kennan, *Memoirs 1925–1950* (Little, Brown and Company, 1967), 258.

12. Truman, *Memoirs*, 341.

13. John Kenneth Galbraith, "The 'Cure' at Mondorf Spa. How Nazi War Criminals lived in Luxembourg Jail," *Life*, October 22, 1945, 18.

14. Erika Mann, "Alien Homeland," Münchner Stadtbibliothek/Monacensia, Nachl. Erika Mann/Manuskripte, EM M 84.

15. Ibid.

16. Elke Fröhlich, ed., *Die Tagebücher von Joseph Goebbels*, Part I, Vol. 2/III (K.G. Saur, 2006), 211.

17. John E. Dolibois, *Pattern of Circles: An Ambassador's Story* (Kent State University Press, 1989), 85.

18. Joachim C. Fest, *Das Gesicht des Dritten Reiches. Profile einer totalitären Herrschaft* (R. Piper & Co., 1988), 246.

19. Dolibois, *Pattern of Circles*, 131.

20. *Der Stürmer*, Nr. 35, August 1925.

21. *Der Stürmer*, Nr. 28, July 1926.

22. Jay W. Baird, "Das politische Testament Julius Streichers. Ein Dokument aus den Papieren des Hauptmanns Dolibois," *Vierteljahreshefte für Zeitgeschichte,* Heft 4/1978, p. 693.

23. Anna Zanco Prestel, ed., *Erika Mann. Briefe und Antworten,* vol. 1 (Edition Spangenberg, 1984), 207.

24. Baird, "Das politische Testament Julius Streichers," 664.

25. Studs Terkel, "One hell of a big bang," *The Guardian,* August 6, 2002.

26. Ibid.

27. Ibid.

28. Michihiko Hachiya, *Hiroshima Diary: The Journal of a Japanese Physician August 6– September 30, 1945* (University of North Carolina Press, 1955), 1–2.

29. Truman, *Memoirs,* 352.

30. White House press release, August 6, 1945, Harry S. Truman Library & Museum.

31. Truman, *Memoirs,* 359.

32. Alfred Misselhorn, *Kriegsende und Gefangenschaft.*

33. Hauptamt für Statistik Gross-Berlin, *Zahlen zeigen Zeitgeschehen,* 10, 18.

34. "Words of Tennô," *KAGAMI,* Neue Folge, edition XVI, issues 1 and 2, Hamburg 1989, p. 107 f.

35. Truman, *Memoirs,* 368.

36. Ibid., 368.

37. Alfred Eisenstaedt, *The Eye of Eisenstaedt* (Viking Press, 1969), 56.

38. Alfred Misselhorn, *Kriegsende und Gefangenschaft.*

39. Andreas-Friedrich, *Schauplatz Berlin,* 98.

40. Ibid., 98n.

41. Ibid., 99.

42. Riess, *Das war ein Leben,* 327.

43. Chamberlin, *Kultur auf Trümmern*, 101.

44. David Niven, *Bring on the Empty Horses* (Putnam, 1975), 146.

45. Deutsches Tagebucharchiv Emmendingen, DTA 2211–1, p. 27.

46. Albrecht Joseph, "Werfel, Alma, Kokoschka, the actor George," p. 33, William-Melnitz-Collection, University of California in Los Angeles, Charles E. Young Research Library.

47. Ibid., 34.

48. Ibid., 34.

49. Cyrill Fischer to Alma Mahler-Werfel, December 15, 1943, Mahler-Werfel-Collection, University of Pennsylvania in Philadelphia, Kislak Center for Special Collections, Rare Books and Manuscripts.

50. Interview by Peter Stephan Jungk with Marta Feuchtwanger, Mechitaristenkloster Wien, Bibliothek, Depositum Peter Stephan Jungk.

51. Adolf Klarmann, Notizbuch, Klarmann-Werfel-Collection, University of Pennsylvania in Philadelphia, Kislak Center for Special Collections, Rare Books and Manuscripts.

52. Mann, *Tagebücher. 1944–1.4.1946*, 247.

53. Igor Stravinsky and Robert Craft, *Expositions and Developments* (University of California Press, 1981), 78.

54. Hauptamt für Statistik Gross-Berlin, *Zahlen zeigen Zeitgeschehen*, 10, 92.

55. Toshikazu Kase, *Journey to the Missouri* (Yale University Press, 1950), 7.

56. "General Douglas MacArthur's Speech at the Surrender of Japan," Papers of Richmond K. Turner, Archives Branch, Naval History and Heritage Command, Washington, DC.

57. Ibid.

58. Kase, *Journey To The Missouri*, 10.

59. "Rhythm in Berlin," *Time Magazine*, September 10, 1945.

60. Chamberlin, *Kultur auf Trümmern*, 142.

61. "Rhythm in Berlin," *Time Magazine.*

62. Thomas Mann, *Tagebücher. 1918–1921*, ed. Peter de Mendelssohn (S. Fischer,1979), 555.

63. Mann, *Tagebücher. 1940–1943*, ed. Peter de Mendelssohn (S. Fischer, 1982), 5.

64. J. F. G. Grosser, ed., *Die große Kontroverse. Ein Briefwechsel um Deutschland* (Nagel, 1963), 18n.

65. Kaspar Hauser [Kurt Tucholsky], "Büchertisch," *Die Weltbühne*, November 24, 1925, 803.

66. Mann, *Tagebücher. 1944–1.4.1946*, 249.

67. Ibid., 250.

68. Thomas Mann, "Brief nach Deutschland," *Essays VI 1945–1950. Große kommentierte Frankfurter Ausgabe*, Vol. 19.1 (S. Fischer, 2009), 72–82.

69. "They all": Thomas Mann to Emil Preetorius, 14 January–24 February 1946. The original letter is held at the University of California, Berkeley, Hargrove Music Library, Alfred Einstein Papers.

70. Torberg, *Liebste Freundin und Alma*, 248.

71. Ibid., 261.

72. Ibid., 212n.

73. Interview with Marietta Torberg, 1987, on the Austrian broadcaster ORF.

74. Spender, *European Witness*, 156n.

75. Ibid., 157.

76. Ibid., 158.

77. Konrad Adenauer, *Erinnerungen 1945–1953* (Deutsche Verlags Anstalt, 1965), 34.

78. Charles Fergusson, memorandum, The National Archives, FO 1013/701.

79. Hans Peter Mensing, "'Dass sich die Fama auch meiner mysteriösen Angelegenheit bemächtigt hat.' Neues zur Entlassung Adenauers als Kölner Nachkriegsoberbürgermeister im Herbst 1945," *Geschichte im Westen*, vol. 1 (1988): 97.

80. Adenauer, *Erinnerungen 1945–1953*, 36n.

81. Hauptamt für Statistik Gross-Berlin, *Zahlen zeigen Zeitgeschehen*, 39.

82. Hans-Peter Schwarz, *Adenauer. Der Aufstieg 1876–1952* (Deutsche Verlags-Anstalt, 1986), 477.

83. Michael Thomas, *Deutschland, England über alles. Rückkehr als Besatzungsoffizier* (Siedler Verlag, 1984), 136.

84. Ibid., 137.

ARCHIVES AND COLLECTIONS

Churchill Archives Centre, Cambridge

CHAR 20/128/27-28: Winston Churchill to Clement Attlee and Anthony Eden, May 21, 1943

Deutsches Tagebucharchiv Emmendingen

DTA 1457-1: Else Tietze, Berlin diary entries, April to August 1945

DTA 2211-1: Annemarie and Johann Hermann von Duhn, Report on their experiences in Berlin in the summer of 1945

Harry S. Truman Library & Museum

The Decision to Drop the Atomic Bomb: Leslie R. Groves and Henry Stimson, July 18, 1945

Oral History Interview with R. Gordon Arneson, Washington, D. C., June 21, 1989

Press release by the White House, August 6, 1945

Landesarchiv Berlin

A Pr. Br. Rep. 030-03 Nr. 1488: Investigation file Gustav Senftleben

A Pr. Br. Rep. 030-03 Nr. 1505: Investigation file Hans Falke

A Pr. Br. Rep. 030-03 Nr. 1545: Investigation file Hans Falke

A Pr. Br. Rep. 030-03 Nr. 1558: Investigation file Body found; victim unknown

F Rep. 280 Nr. 2790: Reopening of restaurants and company kitchens, July 15, 1945

Library of Congress, Washington, D.C.

George S. Patton Papers: Diaries, 1910–1945, Annotated transcripts 1943–1945

Mechitaristenkloster Wien

Library, Depositum Peter Stephan Jungk: Interview Peter Stephan Jungk with Marta Feuchtwanger

Münchner Stadtbibliothek, Monacensia

Erika Mann papers, manuscripts, EM M 84: Alien Homeland

The National Archives, Kew

CAB 65/50/22: War Cabinet, 59th Conclusions, May 7, 1945

FO 954/9B/553: Foreign Office telegram to Paris, No 916

FO 1013/701: German Officials, Dr. Adenauer

Naval History and Heritage Command, Washington, D.C., Archives Branch

Coll/575: Papers of Richmond K. Turner, Box 33, General Douglas MacArthur's Speech at the Surrender of Japan

University of California, Berkeley, Hargrove Music Library
Alfred Einstein Papers

University of California in Los Angeles, Charles E. Young Research Library
William Melnitz Collection

University of Pennsylvania in Philadelphia, Kislak Center for Special Collections, Rare Books and Manuscripts
Klarmann-Werfel Collection
Mahler-Werfel Collection

Internet sources
Deutmann, Karl: *Berlin 1945*, in LeMO-Zeitzeugen, Lebendiges Museum Online, Stiftung Haus der Geschichte der Bundesrepublik Deutschland.
Deutmann, Karl: *Black market in Berlin*, in LeMO-Zeitzeugen, Lebendiges Museum Online, Stiftung Haus der Geschichte der Bundesrepublik Deutschland.
Misselhorn, Alfred: *End of the war and captivity*, in LeMO-Zeitzeugen, Lebendiges Museum Online, Stiftung Haus der Geschichte der Bundesrepublik Deutschland.

Film documents
Interview with Marietta Torberg, 1987, Austrian Broadcasting Corporation.
Freed, Fred: *The Decision to Drop the Bomb*, documentary 1965.
Syberberg, Hans Jürgen: *Winifred Wagner and the history of the Wahnfried House 1914–1975*, documentary 1975.

BIBLIOGRAPHY

Adams, Frank S. "Germany Surrenders. New Yorkers Massed Under Symbol Of Liberty." *New York Times*, May 8, 1945.

Adenauer, Konrad. *Erinnerungen 1945–1953*. Deutsche Verlags Anstalt, 1965.

Allilujewa, Swetlana. *Zwanzig Briefe an einen Freund*. Verlag Fritz Molden, 1967.

Amtsblatt des Kontrollrats in Deutschland, Ergänzungsblatt Nr. 1. Eigenverlag, 1946.

Andreas-Friedrich, Ruth. *Schauplatz Berlin. Tagebuchaufzeichnungen 1945–1948*. Suhrkamp, 1986.

Andrus, Burton C. *The Infamous of Nuremberg*. Leslie Frewin, 1969.

Anonymous [Marta Hillers]. *Eine Frau in Berlin. Tagebuch-Aufzeichnungen vom 20. April bis 22. June 1945*. btb, 2008.

Assmann, Michael, ed. *Thomas Mann, Erich von Kahler. Briefwechsel 1931–1955*. Luchterhand Literaturverlag 1993.

Bainbridge, Kenneth T. "'All in our Time.' A foul and awesome display," in *Bulletin of the Atomic Scientists* (May 1975), 40–46.

Baird, Jay W. "Das politische Testament Julius Streichers. Ein Dokument aus den Papieren des Hauptmanns Dolibois," *Vierteljahreshefte für Zeitgeschichte*, vol. 4 (1978): 660–693.
"Baptism by Desire." *New York Times*, April 29, 1990, p. BR15.
Beachy, Robert. *Gay Berlin: Birthplace of a modern identity.* Vintage, 2015.
Bermann Fischer, Gottfried. *Bedroht—bewahrt. Der Weg eines Verlegers.* Fischer, 1982.
Bermann Fischer, Gottfried. *Wanderer durch ein Jahrhundert.* Fischer, 1994.
Beyer, Marion, Jürgen May, and Walter Werbeck, eds. *Richard Strauss. Späte Aufzeichnungen.* Schott Music, 2016.
Brett-Smith, Richard. *Berlin '45. The Grey City.* Macmillan, 1966.
Burger, Hanuš. *Der Frühling war es wert. Erinnerungen.* Ullsetin, 1977.
Chamberlin, Brewster S. *Kultur auf Trümmern. Berliner Berichte der amerikanischen Information Control Section Juli–Dezember 1945.* Deutsche Verlags-Anstalt, 1979.
Churchill, Winston S. *The Second World War. Triumph and Tragedy.* Houghton Mifflin Company, 1953.
Clay, Lucius D. *Decision in Germany.* Doubleday, 1950.
Colville, John. *The Fringes of Power. Downing Street Diaries 1939–1955.* Hodder and Stoughton, 1985.
Cooper, Diana. *Trumpets from the Steep.* Rupert Hart-Davis, 1960.
Cooper, Duff. *Old Men Forget.* E. P. Dutton & Co., Inc., 1954.
Dallas, Gregor. *1945. The war that never ended.* Yale University Press, 2005.
Dilks, David, ed. *The Diaries of Sir Alexander Cadogan 1938–1945.* Cassell, 1971.
Döblin, Alfred. *Ausgewählte Werke*, Vol. 13: *Briefe.* Walter Verlag, 1970.

Dolibois, John E. *Pattern of Circles. An Ambassador's Story*. Kent State University Press, 1989.

Ehrsam, Thomas, and Regula Wyss, eds. *Thea Sternheim. Tagebücher 1903–1971*, vol. 3. Wallsetin Verlag 2002.

Eisenstaedt, Alfred. *The Eye of Eisenstaedt*. Viking Press, 1969.

Ferrell, Robert H., ed. *Dear Bess. The letters from Harry to Bess Truman 1910–1959*, W. W. Norton & Company, 1983.

Fest, Joachim C. *Das Gesicht des Dritten Reiches. Profile einer totalitären Herrschaft*. R. Piper & Co., 1988.

Fischer, Alexander, ed. *Teheran, Jalta, Potsdam. Die sowjetischen Protokolle von den Kriegskonferenzen der "Großen Drei."* Wissenschaft, 1968.

Foreign Relations of the United States. Diplomatic Papers, The Conference of Berlin 1945, 2 vol. 1. United States Government Printing Office, 1960.

Friedländer, Margot. *"Versuche dein Leben zu machen." Als Jüdin versteckt in Berlin*. Rowohlt, 2008.

Fröhlich, Elke, ed. *Die Tagebücher von Joseph Goebbels*, Teil I, Bd. 2/III. K.G. Saur, 2006.

Galbraith, John Kenneth. "'The Cure' at Mondorf Spa. How Nazi War Criminals lived in Luxembourg Jail," in: *Life*, October 22, 1945.

Gaulle, Charles de. *Discours et Messages. Pendant la guerre, Juin 1940–Janvier 1946*. Plon, 1970.

Gilbert, Martin. *The Day the War Ended. VE-Day 1945 in Europe and Around the World*. Henry Holt & Co., 1995.

Görlitz, Walter, ed. *Generalfeldmarschall Keitel—Verbrecher oder Offizier? Erinnerungen, Briefe, Dokumente des Chefs OKW*. Musterschmidt Verlag, 1961.

Gromyko, Andrei. *Memoirs*. Doubleday, 1989.

Grosser, J. F. G., ed. *Die große Kontroverse. Ein Briefwechsel um Deutschland*. Nagel, 1963.

Hauptamt für Statistik Gross-Berlin, ed. *Zahlen zeigen Zeitgeschehen. Berlin 1945–1947*. Hauptamt für Statistik Gross-Berlin,1947.

Hauser, Kaspar [d. i. Kurt Tucholsky]. "Büchertisch," *Die Weltbühne*. November 24, 1925.

Hauser, Kaspar [d. i. Kurt Tucholsky]. "Die lieben Kinder," *Die Weltbühne*. February 19, 1929.

Henke, Klaus-Dietmar. *Die amerikanische Besetzung Deutschlands*. De Gruyter Oldenbourg, 1996.

"Hungernde deutsche Mädchen in den Klauen geiler Judenböcke," *Der Stürmer*, Nr. 35, August 1925.

Iken, Katja, Uwe Klußmann and Eva-Maria Schnurr, eds. *Als Deutschland sich neu erfand. Die Nachkriegszeit 1945–1949*. Penguin, 2019.

James, Robert Rhodes, ed. *Winston S. Churchill. His complete speeches*, vol. 7. Chelsea House Publishers, 1974.

Lubrich, Oliver, ed. *John F. Kennedy's Hidden Diary, Europe 1937. The Travel Journals of JFK and Kirk Lemoyne Billings*. Berghahn Books, 2023.

Jungk, Peter Stephan. *Franz Werfel. Eine Lebensgeschichte*. S. Fischer, 1987.

Kästner, Erich. *Notabene 45. Ein Tagebuch*. Atrium, 2017.

Karasek, Hellmuth. *Billy Wilder. Eine Nahaufnahme*. Hoffman und Campe, 2006.

Kase, Toshikazu. *Journey To The Missouri*. Yale University Press, 1950.

Kennan, George F. *Memoirs 1925–1950*. Little, Brown and Company, 1967.

Lamont, Lansing. *Day of Trinity*. Atheneum, 1965.

Leahy, William D. *I was there. The personal story of the chief of staff to Presidents Roosevelt and Truman based on his notes and diaries made at the time.* Whittlesey House, 1950.

Lehndorff, Hans von. *Ostpreußisches Tagebuch. Aufzeichnungen eines Arztes aus den Jahren 1945–1947.* dtv, 1967.

Mann, Klaus. *The Turning Point: Thirty-five Years in This Century* (L. B. Fischer, 1942).

Mann, Thomas. *Briefe III, 1924–1932* (S. Fischer Verlag, 2011).

Mann, Thomas. "Brief nach Deutschland," in Thomas Mann, *Essays VI 1945–1950.* Große kommentierte Frankfurter Ausgabe, Bd. 19.1. S. Fischer, 2009.

Mann, Thomas. *Tagebücher. 1918–1921,* Peter de Mendelssohn. S. Fischer, 1979.

Mann, Thomas. *Tagebücher. 1937–1939,* Peter de Mendelssohn. S. Fischer, 1980.

Mann, Thomas. *Tagebücher. 1940–1943,* Peter de Mendelssohn. S. Fischer, 1982.

Mann, Thomas. *Tagebücher. 1944–1.4.1946,* ed. Inge Jens. S. Fischer, 1986.

Mark, Eduard. "'Today Has Been A Historical One.' Harry S. Truman's Diary of the Potsdam Conference," *Diplomatic History,* vol. 4, issue 3 (July 1980).

Mensing, Hans Peter. "'Dass sich die Fama auch meiner mysteriösen Angelegenheit bemächtigt hat.' Neues zur Entlassung Adenauers als Kölner Nachkriegsoberbürgermeister im Herbst 1945," in *Geschichte im Westen,* vol. 1 (1988): 84–98.

Mira, Brigitte. *Kleine Frau—was nun? Erinnerungen an ein buntes Leben.* Ullstein Verlag, 1988.

Montefiore, Simon Sebag. *Stalin. Am Hof des roten Zaren.* S. Fischer, 2005.

Moran, Baron (Charles McMoran Wilson). *Winston Churchill: Struggle For Survival 1945–1960.* Constable, 1966.

Muck, Peter. *Einhundert Jahre Berliner Philharmonisches Orchester. Darstellung in Dokumenten*, vol. 2. H. Schneider, 1982.
Niven, David. *Bring on the Empty Horses*. Putnam, 1975.
Norwich, John Julius, ed. *The Duff Cooper Diaries, 1915–1951*. Phoenix, 2005.
Padover, Saul K. *Experiment in Germany*. Duell, Sloan & Pearce, 1946.
Poen, Monte M., ed. *Letters Home by Harry Truman*. G. P. Putnam's Sons, 1984.
Ramsey, Winston G. "Himmler's Suicide," *After the Battle*, Nr. 14, 15. August 1976.
"Rhythm in Berlin." *Time Magazine*, September 10, 1945.
Riess, Curt. *Das war ein Leben! Erinnerungen*. Albert Langen, 1986.
"Ritualmord? Wer ist der Kinderschlächter von Breslau?," *Der Stürmer*, Nr. 28. July 1926.
Rösch, Gertrud Maria. "'I thought it wiser not to disclose my identity.' Die Begegnung zwischen Klaus Mann und Richard Strauss im Mai 1945," in *Thomas Mann Jahrbuch*, Vol. 14, Tutzing 2001, pp. 233–248.
Schaeffers, Willi. *Tingeltangel. Ein Leben für die Kleinkunst*. Broschek, 1959.
Scherstjanoi, Elke, ed. *Rotarmisten schreiben aus Deutschland. Briefe von der Front (1945) und historische Analysen*. De Gruyter Saur, 2004.
Schwarz, Hans-Peter. *Adenauer. Der Aufstieg 1876–1952*. Deutsche Verlags-Anstalt, 1986.
Shirer, William L. *The End of a Berlin Diary*. Popular Library, 1961.
Sidey, Hugh, ed. *Prelude to Leadership. The European Diary of John F. Kennedy Summer 1945*. Regnery Pub, 1995.
Simonow, Konstantin. *Kriegstagebücher 1942–1945*. Kindler Verlag, 1982.

Spender, Stephen. *European Witness.* Hamish Hamilton Ltd., 1946.
Stalin, Josef. *Reden, Interviews, Telegramme, Befehle, Briefe und Botschaften. Mai 1945 – Oktober 1952.* Parteihochschule Karl Marx, 1952.
Stalin, Josef. *Über den großen vaterländischen Krieg der Sowjetunion,* Berlin 1952.
Stalin's Correspondence with Churchill, Attlee, Roosevelt and Truman 1941–45. E.P. Dutton & Co., Inc. 1958.
Stemann, Paul van. "Himmler's Night of Reckoning," *Independent,* May 20, 1995.
Sträßner, Matthias. *Leo Borchard. Eine unvollendete Karriere,* Berlin 1999.
Stravinsky, Igor, and Robert Craft. *Expositions and Developments.* University of California Press, 1981.
Symonette, Lys and Kim H. Kowalke, eds. *Speak Low when you speak love. The Letters of Kurt Weill and Lotte Lenya.* University of California Press, 1996.
Terkel, Studs. "One hell of a big bang." *The Guardian,* August 6, 2002.
Thomas, Michael. *Deutschland, England über alles. Rückkehr als Besatzungsoffizier.* Siedler Verlag, 1984.
Torberg, Friedrich. *Liebste Freundin und Alma. Briefwechsel mit Alma Mahler-Werfel.* Ullstein 1987.
Truman, Harry S. *Memoirs. Vol. 1, The Year of Decisions.* Doubleday, 1955.
Truman, Margaret. *Harry S. Truman.* Morrow, 1973.
Vaget, Hans Rudolf, ed. *Thomas Mann, Agnes E. Meyer. Briefwechsel 1937–1955.* S. Fischer, 1992.
Vaget, Hans Rudolf. *Thomas Mann, der Amerikaner.* S. Fischer, 2012.
Werth, Alexander. *Russia at War 1941–1945.* Skyhorse, 1964.

Wolkogonow, Dimitri. *Stalin, Triumph und Tragödie. Ein politisches Porträt*. Claassen, 1989.

"Worte des Tennô," in *KAGAMI*, Neue Folge, Jahrgang XVI, Vol. 1 and 2, Hamburg 1989, pp. 100–111.

Zanco Prestel, Anna. *Erika Mann. Briefe und Antworten*, vol. 1. Edition Spangenberg, 1984.

Zellermayer, Heinz M. *Alles zu meiner Zeit. Tagebuch-Erinnerungen an ein reiches Leben zwischen Gastlichkeit, Politik und Kunst*. Arne, 1990.

Zellermayer, Ilse. *Drei Tenöre und ein Sopran. Mein Leben für die Oper*. Henschel, 2000.

Zhukow, Georgi K. *Reminiscences and Reflections*, vol. 2. Progress Publishers, 1985.

IMAGE CREDITS

p. viii Hensky, Herbert (1910–2005) © Copyright bpk. Hitler bust in the rubble at the Potsdamer Brücke in Mitte, Berlin, 1946. Photo credit: bpk Bildagentur / Art Resource, NY.

p. 4 Corbis Historical / Getty Images.

p. 28 Niday Picture Library / Alamy.

p. 37 Hubmann, Hanns (1910–1996) © Copyright bpk. Richard Strauss at the piano in his house with his son, 1945, Garmisch-Partenkirchen. Photo credit: bpk Bildagentur / Art Resource, NY.

p. 40 ullsteinbild / TopFoto.

p. 52 © Copyright bpk. A destroyed apartment in a severely damaged building serves as an emergency balcony in the summer. Berlin, 1946. Photo credit: bpk Bildagentur / Art Resource, NY.

p. 56 ullstein bild / Getty Images.

p. 66 akg-images / Voller Ernst / Chaldej.

p. 76 Bettmann / Getty Images.

p. 87 Alma Mahler Production, Vienna.

p. 100 © Copyright bpk. Black Market and Barter Market at the Brandenburg Gate with Russian Sailors and Soldiers, 1945. Photo credit: bpk Bildagentur / Art Resource, NY.

p. 104 Shawshots / Alamy.

p. 114 akg-images / Voller Ernst / Chaldej.

p. 131 akg-images / Voller Ernst / Chaldej.

p. 133 Wikipedia Commons.

p. 146 Wikipedia Commons.

p. 155 GK History Images / Alamy.

p. 164 Everett Collection Inc / Alamy.

p. 168 Ezra Stoller / Esto.

p. 196 Alfred Eisenstaedt / The LIFE Picture Collection / Shutterstock.

p. 201 Hensky, Herbert (1910–2005) © Copyright bpk. Rubble Women (at Straußberger Platz in the Friedrichshain district, Berlin), 1946. Photo credit: bpk Bildagentur / Art Resource, NY.

p. 204 Ralph Crane / The LIFE Picture Collection / Shutterstock.

p. 214 Pictorial Press Ltd / Alamy.

p. 226 piemags/ww2archive / Alamy.

p. 233 United Archives GmbH / Alamy.